Shattered REALITY

LISAMARIE KADE

Shattered Reality
The Red Society
Book Two

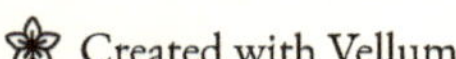 Created with Vellum

Note to readers

This book contains topics that may be sensitive to some.

*Past childhood trauma /abuse
*alcoholism
While the story does not go into specific detail of abuse, it is still mentioned.

Chapter One
SCARLETT

My name is Scarlett Ward, and this is my story.

I sigh, looking into the mirror. My makeup is in place, hiding the dark circles that threaten to appear. My eyes look beyond tired. Truth be told, I am. I'm sick of my mom's shit. Sick of her problems. I'm sick of working this fucking job, just to take care of my mom's bullshit. It's not fair and it sucks. Yet I keep doing it. Why? Hell if I know some days. Other days, though, I feel I owe it to her.

"Hey Lettie, you're almost up."

"Thanks, Marc."

Time to plaster on my fake smile and give the gents what they came here for. I finish strapping on my sky-high heels and head out.

When I take the stage, I usually don't notice the men. I try to focus on the lights, the liquor bottles on the shelf behind the bar. Anything but the men.

Tonight is different though. I notice him right away as

he walks with a purpose. I follow his movements while continuing to dance. He takes his place in the VIP section. No surprise. He looks like the type that belongs in the VIP of any and everything. Perfectly styled hair, suit pressed. Yeah, he oozes money.

The minute he glances my way, I tense slightly. I don't know why. Maybe it is because when I look back at the mystery man, he is still staring. I'm confident up here. I've been dancing since I was sixteen. I'm twenty-four now, and I know how to own the stage. Even when I look away, I can still feel his eyes all over my body. *Duh, Scarlett. You are basically naked.*

Taking my time, I dance around the huge pole that is placed near the front of the stage. For some unknown reason, men love seeing a woman wrapped around a pole. Like clockwork, the hollering starts. I pop my ass out, teasing those close to the stage.

When I come around again, my eyes betray me, seeking the handsome man out. He is still staring at me. I should be worried, except I'm not. Here is where I am safe. Mr. Sinclair keeps all his employees safe. Top security and cameras everywhere.

For a moment I wonder if my mother owes him money. Then shake away those thoughts. He is too clean-cut and proper; my mother seems to only know how to deal with low-life scum. A man of his magnitude would never bother with my mother. Hell, I wouldn't even bother with her if I didn't have to.

As soon as the second song starts, I know my time is about up. That means it's crunch time to earn dollar bills. I wink once as I take off my red bra. My nipples are covered by nothing but black tape. Like always, it's a crowd pleaser. Money is thrown on stage. Money. The reason I work here.

When the song ends, I give my signature smile and blow the crowd a sexy little air kiss. They go wild, and part of me dies inside every time they do. Are they all like this? Yes, yes, they are. As I saunter my way off stage, Marc pulls me aside.

"You've been requested."

"I have?"

His words shock me. I'm not usually requested. It rarely happens, and I'm just fine with that even if the money is triple what stage money is. His face gives nothing else away while he continues to stare at the tablet. Watching the cameras, I assume.

"I'll give you five to get ready."

Shit! I nod before turning to run back to the dressing room. Five minutes. That's not a whole lot of time to freshen up. I need to reapply deodorant, spray some more perfume, and blot the sweat from my face. Maybe if I'm lucky, I'll have time to reapply my lipstick too.

Five minutes is not even enough time to change. Whoever requested me will have to take me exactly as I was on stage. I groan out as I pull my necessities out of my bag.

"What's wrong, Lettie?" Tia asks.

Tia is another dancer. She's been here maybe a year or so, give or take. She's nice. All the dancers are nice, but I hold them at arm's length. I don't have time for real friendships. It's not like I can bring them back to my place to hang out.

"I've been requested, and Marc only gave me five minutes."

"Damn girl, better hurry."

I DON'T BOTHER with a response. There's no time. I'm anxious and rushing to apply a new shade of lipstick. Bubblegum pink. I stand back, looking myself over in the brightly lit mirror. *This will have to do.* I really hope it's enough to please whoever wants me.

"Let's go, Lettie." Marc's voice comes over the intercom and the room goes silent. Eyes look at me through their mirrors. I grab a hair clip off the counter, pinning my hair up. I don't have time to explain, nor will I when I get back. I owe these dancers nothing. I've been here the longest. That's a depressing fact, nevertheless, it's a fact.

Holding my head high, I march my ass right out the door to find Marc waiting. He looks bored and says nothing as he starts walking.

I follow him to the private area of the club. The private lounge is behind the scenes and away from prying eyes. The music is much softer on this side of the club. People can actually have conversations without the music vibrating through their souls.

We slow down, and I feel my heart rate pick up slightly as we reach the crimson red doors. Who is on the other side and why did they choose me?

Chapter Two

SPENCER

GRABBING my drink off the bar, I turn toward the stage. A new song has started and that means there's a new dancer. I take her in from the clear heels on her feet, following her slender legs up to her thighs. I watch as her ass shakes in the g-string she's wearing. Not too bad. Her stomach is flat and slightly toned. My eyes can't help but pause at her chest. Her tits are all but spilling out of the red bra thing she has on. It matches her plump lips. Her blonde hair falls over her shoulders as she works the stage. I won't lie, it makes my dick twitch slightly. I wouldn't mind those lips wrapped around it.

Shaking my head, I start to make my way back to my Charla. I don't know why my eyes keep finding my way back to the dancer on stage. I tell myself it is because I'm a guy and she is sexy to watch.

"Earth to Spence."

"Yeah, sorry." I look at Charla who has one brow raised and a smirk on her face. She caught me staring at the stripper.

"I see you." She laughs at me while shaking her head.

I say nothing, just take a swig of my rum and coke while glancing back toward the stage. The dancer is now slowly dancing up and down the pole. She starts removing her bra. Tiny black X's cover her nipples. My eyes focus on them and nothing else. All the chatter in the room is just background noise now. Her tits are perfect. So fucking round, just the right size too.

She continues dancing and it's mesmerizing to watch. The way her hips sway, how her breasts bounce every time she squats while popping her ass. It's a turn on and I can't help but picture her on top of me naked, bouncing on my cock in the same motion. Just the thought has my hard cock straining painfully in my slacks.

"Why don't you request some VIP treatment?" Charla's voice pulls me back to the present once again. It annoys me, yet I don't let it show.

"Nah, I'm good."

Her eyes flick down to where my erection is clearly evident. Charla has no shame. It's a good thing she is my best friend, otherwise I'd drag her to a dark hallway and punish her for being so blunt.

"Little Worthington wants some attention though."

"What? Don't call my cock that." Seriously, the girl needs to be punished. Just not by me.

Charla throws her head back, laughing, and her long blonde hair falls back from her face. She's beautiful and she knows it. Completely off limits, still she's beautiful.

Once she regains her composure, she stands and straightens the navy skintight skirt she has on. At the same time, the music fades out and the dancer disappears behind the red velvet curtain. Thank fuck because I was really considering going after her and that's not like me. I've never been desperate for pussy.

"Excuse me." Charla nods her head once and winks at me.

I have a feeling she's up to something, but I let it go. There's no stopping her, unless it involves her father. That's the only time she is on her best behavior. It's quite sick how he controls her and demands things of her. I've told Charla on more than one occasion that she needs to break free of his controlling ways, but she won't hear it. She feels she owes him everything. Whatever. Not my problem.

A few minutes later Charla returns with a new drink and a pep in her step. She did something. It's written across her face. She sits down across from me with a shit-eating grin on her face.

"You can thank me later."

"For what?"

"You'll see." Her eyes flick behind me and then back to me again. A smirk is plastered on her lips.

The two of us sit in silence for a few minutes. There's a new dancer on stage, dark hair, perfect curves, but she doesn't interest me. Not in the way the blonde did. I even try to focus on her ass. Nope, doesn't affect me in the same way.

"Mr. Worthington?" a male's voice booms from behind me. I turn to see a man a little taller than me. He's in a dark dress shirt with sleeves rolled up. His arms are covered in tattoos.

"That's me," I state, sitting up straighter, hoping to shoo this guy on his way. I don't entertain people like him and really don't care about what he wants from me. I'm used to this. People come to me all the time for hand out. Just because I'm successful. Not today though. I'm not that guy.

"You've requested Lettie in the gold lounge, she'll be ready in a few minutes." The guy squints at me as if he is trying to figure me out and I don't like it. Not one bit.

"I'm sorry?"

I wait while the guy looks at his phone for a few seconds before acknowledging me. When he looks back up he looks past me to Charla, and that doesn't sit right with me.

"Excuse me, I'm over here."

Drawing his attention back to me he says, "Yes, it seems your friend here," he glances back at Charla, "treated you to some extra VIP treatment with one of my dancers. Take it or leave it."

The minute that last bit leaves his mouth his eyes are back on Charla. I turn to question her, but she is staring at him in the same fashion. What in the fresh hell is this? There's no way she's interested in this dude.

"Charla?"

She immediately breaks eye contact with him and looks at me.

"I figured you might enjoy a little show." She shrugs her shoulders like it's no big deal.

"If you'll follow me, I'll show you to the lounge."

"Yeah, sure." I take one last swig of my drink and slide out of the booth. Charla is in some deep shit for this stunt and even more for checking out this punk's ass as he walks away.

I start following and catch him looking back over his

shoulder toward Charla more than once. I should tell him to keep his eyes off her. She's way out of his league. I don't. I decide to let the fool wish he could have someone like her.

"Does your girlfriend allow you to be with other women often?"

I'm baffled. "Dude, what?"

"Your girlfriend, does she always pay for these types of services?"

"She's not my girlfriend first off and if she was, it's none of your business." Something about this guy rubs me the wrong way. He says nothing until we come to a set of dark red doors. He pulls out a key and sticks it in the hole but doesn't turn the lock. Instead, he turns to look at me.

"You will be respectful to Lettie. There's to be no touching her whatsoever. You touch her and you'll be thrown out so fast, along with a broken nose."

He can't be serious, there's no way he is calling me scum. I glare back at him.

In one swift move, he's moved away from the door and is now inches from my face.

"I'm dead serious, Worthington. We don't play around here. I run a tight ship and have no time for preppy assholes who think they are entitled to women." He swallows slowly before continuing, "So if you think you are entitled and that my rules don't apply, I think it would be wise of you to turn around and go back to that girl out there."

He's the boss?!

As much as I hate to admit, I respect that guy for taking his job seriously, although he went about it the wrong way. It's not like I plan to touch any of these chicks anyway. *Nope, just dream about the one dancer fucking me.*

"Got it."

"Good, shall we?"

I don't bother with a response, just a nod.

The guy opens the door and calls for a woman named Lettie. When there's no response, he checks his phone before looking at me.

"She'll be here in just a minute, they are coming up now."

"They?" I ask, confused. Does he mean more than one stripper?

"The bodyguard and Lettie. I do not allow my employees to move through the club without support. Too many pricks."

"Understandable." I respect him a little more now that he values the women as more than just strippers.

"What's your name?" I ask mostly because I'm bored, but also there's no way he owns this place. He has to just be head of security or something.

"Sinclair and I already know what you are thinking, that I can't possibly own this place looking the way I do. In fact I do. Shocking, I know."

Well I'll be damned, that was what I was thinking. How on earth is this rough looking guy owning a well-established club such as this?

All thoughts fly out the window when a security guard walks in with the sexy blonde dancer who was on stage earlier. The one who captured my attention is now standing feet away from me in the exact same thing she was wearing on stage. Red lingerie. The only thing different now is her lipstick is pink. It was red when she was on stage. I'm certain of it.

"Lettie, Mr. Worthington has the pleasure of your company for the next forty minutes. Marc will be just outside, should you need his assistance. He will come to collect you in exactly forty minutes."

"Yes, sir," Lettie replies, sounding not so confident, and I wonder if it is because of me or her boss.

"Very well. Enjoy, Mr. Worthington."

I stand there as he and the guard turn and leave. I hear the lock turn once they are on the other side. Odd.

"It's for me, I mean the dancer's protection. It's so men can't lock themselves in here with the dancers. Only the guards and Mr. Sinclair have keys."

"I'm impressed." The guy has thought of everything to keep this place smooth sailing.

The woman studies me for a moment. She pulls her bottom lip in between her teeth before making eye contact with me and that's when I know I'm in trouble. Forty minutes of her and no touching her in places that my dick already wants to touch her is going to be pure torture.

Fucking Charla and her games.

Chapter Three

SCARLETT

Marc closes and locks the doors, leaving us alone. It makes me feel vulnerable. I don't know why, it just feels different with him. There's something in the way he looks at me. The oh-so-handsome mystery man stands in front of me, hands in his front pockets. He looked good from afar, but damn he is fucking hot up close. It should be a sin. Dark hair and vibrant green eyes. No stubble on his face. I bet he shaves it every single day.

Mystery man clears his throat, pulling me from thoughts. I smile through my nervousness. *You can do this, Scarlett.*

"I'm Lettie, it's a pleasure to serve you."

"Mr. Worthington." His deep voice vibrates off the walls. "Shall we?"

I nod once. "We shall." I hold my hand out for him to take so I can escort him to a chaise lounge while silently praying that he can't feel me trembling.

When he doesn't take my hand, I look up at him.

"No touching. It is part of the rules," he says cautiously.

"Right, okay then."

I find myself at his staring hands. Strong hands that don't look like they've ever done any type of hard labor. I pause at a table that holds the Bluetooth speaker and tablet. I need to select music.

"Do you have a preference?"

I don't know why I ask, I have a feeling he doesn't give a damn. He's here for a show and nothing more. I choose a song by Halestorm, "Do Not Disturb." I like my music a little harder than what they play on the main floor. The harder the music, the easier it is to drown out the reality of my life.

Turning, I look at the man in front of me. He's studying me in the same fashion that I am studying him.

"Take your pick." I point past him. There's a black leather armchair and across from it is a large black velvet chaise lounge.

Mr. Worthington turns to look at his options while I grab the remote for the music. I don't care what he chooses, I've given dances on both. The realization makes me sad. I shake it off though, after all I have a job to do.

He makes his way to the armchair and sits down.

"Are you comfortable?"

"Yes, I am, Lettie." The way his deep voice says my name awakens something inside of me. A tingling I haven't felt in years.

I walk close and hit play on the remote before tossing it on the small round table next to his chair. The music starts and I must remind myself that I am here to serve this guy, no time to feel silly things. I'm a professional and will not allow him to affect my performance.

Slowly swaying my hips, I pull the clip out of my hair, allowing it to cascade freely over my shoulders. I make my way closer to him and continue dancing for a minute, getting lost in the music.

Once I feel my confidence rise, I move closer to straddle him. When I do, his green eyes flare and he tilts his head. I grab his dress shirt and very lightly push him back in the chair. Mr. Worthington's eyes drop to my hand fisted in his shirt before glancing up at me. I smile shyly and take note of his hands that are resting on each armrest. Usually, I have to place a man's hands there for my show. All men are the same. Talking dirty to me while grabbing their junk. Not Mr. Worthington though, he seems to be a gentleman so far.

I scoot closer to him, it causes him to tense. I allow myself a few moments to dance on his lap while pushing my chest closer to his face. It's a risky game I'm playing, but I suddenly crave the adrenaline. It's the only thing that reminds me that I am alive.

I am undeniably close to his face, so close I feel his hot breath blow across the bare skin of my neck. I can smell the rum on his breath. For a moment, I wonder what he tastes like.

I can't help but grind to the beat of the music. Hell, if I can't feel how hard I've already made this man. It should gross me out, yet for some reason he doesn't make me feel dirty.

I look up at him and that's when I see it, I see something flash in his green eyes. I look away quickly. His stare was intense and I'm not sure how to process that. I focus on his perfect lips as I continue moving. They do little to distract me from his erection that rubs against me just right. It is starting to stir something inside of me and that's definitely never happened while performing before. And I mean never.

Now I'm far from innocent, being a dancer and all, but I've always been able to keep it professional. The men aren't scum. No, Mr. Sinclair would never let such men into his club. It's always been about making money and nothing more. Besides, it's hard to date doing what I do, let alone have a serious relationship. Plus add my mom and her issues into the equation and there's no point. I've given up on men and relationships. I have my selection of toys that get the job done most days. Right now, though, I want to feel a man inside of me. I shake my head to clear my thoughts. This, whatever I am suddenly feeling, is absolutely nothing.

Halestorm ends and I slowly get off his lap. He exhales loudly. I wonder how long he had been holding his breath.

A more upbeat song starts so I turn away from him, allowing him to watch my ass freely. I'm thankful for the reprieve. Being able to dance without making eye contact with him is just what I need. Even though I can still feel his eyes on me, it's not as intense.

I decide to take my time dancing this way, shaking and popping my ass. I don't consider myself a large girl, in fact, I hate labeling any woman with a size. I like to think of myself as a thick in all the right places type of girl. I have curves and an ass. My ass has gotten me more tips than I care to admit, so I won't complain. My body is what keeps me fed and the bills paid, mostly.

As soon as the song ends, I turn back around to Mr. Worthington's heated glare. It's alarming and almost scary.

"Is everything okay, Mr. Worthington?"

"Yes."

Okay, that's a good response, I think.

"Shall I get you a drink before continuing?"

"Water."

This man continues to surprise me. I smile as I walk to the wet bar. God, I hope there is water in the fridge. No one has ever asked me for a bottle of water before.

Thankfully, when I pull open the door to the mini fridge, there are several bottles of water. I quickly bring it back to the mysterious man. He is paying for my time, and I sure don't want to displease him. He's paying for a show, and I intend to make sure he gets the best.

He takes the water and I watch in silence as his fingers unscrew the cap. As he takes a sip, I watch his Adam's apple bob when he swallows. He looked incredibly sexy. *What in the hell is wrong with me?*

I turn away and grab the remote. I need a distraction. I decide to skip the current song. I can't stand to start performing in the middle of a song. It drives me mad.

"Twisted" by Keith Sweat starts and I turn back to face Mr. Worthington. I immediately feel a shift in the air. He must feel it too. I know he does because he is gripping the armrest so tight that the veins in his hands are clearly evident. Even his veins are sexy. I don't know how, but his are. Yup. I'm officially crazy.

I slowly tease him, leaning my chest straight in his face. Taking a slight step back, I reach back to unhook my bra and very slowly bring the strap down my arm. I do the same with the other side except this time I make the mistake of making eye contact with him. His eyes are trained on my breasts, and I can't be sure, but I think I see something in his eyes. Heat, desire, hell I'm so out of touch with a man I can't be sure.

Mr. Worthington glances up at me and that's when I stop dancing and freeze in place. His stare makes me feel like I'm burning up.

"Mr. Worthington?" I barely whisper, my throat has gone dry.

I watch as he swallows thickly before speaking. "I think you should take a step back."

His deep voice sends chills down my spine. I don't move though, I'm frozen in place. Can't seem to make myself move.

Looking down at his hands, they now have a death grip on the arm rest. It should make me fear him, yet it doesn't.

"I need you to step back now."

My eyes dart back to him and that's when I realize there is a war waging in his eyes. It's written all over his face.

I quickly take two steps back and as soon as I do, he jumps out of the chair and makes a beeline for the door. He stops at it and pulls out his wallet. He says nothing as he walks back toward me. He walks past me, so I turn to see what he is doing. He places money on the table, then storms out of the room without looking back.

What the hell?

Chapter Four

SCARLETT

I stand there stunned and confused. Why did Mr. Worthington suddenly walk out? Was it something I did? I don't understand what just happened.

Fear suddenly invades my thoughts. Mr. Sinclair is going to be so pissed and that means I'll probably miss out on a big tip tonight. Shit. I don't need any setbacks. I have no answers and he is going to want them.

I hear two knocks before Marc walks in with a questioning look.

"Everything all right, Lettie?"

"I don't know, he got up and walked out without saying anything." I shrug my shoulders and look down.

"He didn't harm you, did he?"

"What? No! Of course not. He was surprisingly polite, and I did not have to remind him of the rules."

"Good." Mr. Sinclair's voice startles me as he walks in and around Marc. He comes to stand straight in front of me.

In my early years, I was groped more times than I care

to count. Mr. Sinclair's grandfather never cared. Told us it was part of the job. I hated it. The teenager in me learned to block it all out. All of the gross men. Mr. Sinclair came in and changed all that though. He made new rules. No more men touching any of us without permission. It was a welcomed change for a shit job that I never asked for.

I keep my eyes cast downward. I do not want to see the disappointment in his eyes. I try extremely hard not to make Mr. Sinclair angry. I need this job. My life depends on it.

"Tell me what happened, now." His voice is void of any emotion and that makes it that much worse.

"I don't know, the song came to an end, and I offered him a drink. He chose water. When I selected the next song and came over to his lap, I began to remove my top and that's when he asked me to step back. I did and he was up and gone in less than a minute."

I always go with the truth. I learned a long time ago to never lie to the boss. I've seen my fair share of dancers fired on the spot for lying.

"And he said nothing?"

I look up now. Those piercing eyes of Mr. Sinclair's glare at me. He's confirming my story.

"No, he said nothing aside from asking me to step back."

Mr. Sinclair turns toward Marc.

"Where is he now?"

"He gathered up the lady and they seem to be headed for the exit." Marc holds the tablet up, showing the camera. Sure enough, it's zoomed in on Mr. Worthington and a blonde. He has his arm on the small of her back as he leads her out. How odd that he would be here with a woman and request a private lap dance.

"Maybe he felt guilty having me on his lap with that woman sitting out in the club alone." I point to the camera. It's the only logical thing that would make any sense at this point.

"They aren't an item," Mr. Sinclair all but snaps.

Marc and I give each other a look. Glad I'm not the only one who finds it out of character for the boss to react like that over a woman.

"Now what?" Marc asks.

I watch out of the corner of my eye, too anxious to make eye contact as my boss rubs his chin. He is silent for a few minutes before he finally speaks.

"Disinfect the room and then you may go for the evening. Marc, make sure one of the guys walks her out."

Go for the evening! I glance at the clock on the wall as fear overtakes my mind. I can't. I need the money. There is no way in hell I can go home this early. Mr. Sinclair cannot send me home. I need to speak up.

"Sir, I need to stay. I need the--"

"You'll be paid for the private show. You are to leave as soon as the room is clean."

I nod in relief. "Yes, sir."

I stand there and watch Mr. Sinclair storm out. He doesn't glance back. Not once. Marc nods once at me and then he is gone too, leaving me alone to catch my breath and to calm my racing heart.

I walk to the cabinet in the far corner of the room and grab the disinfectant spray and a disposable cloth. Walking back to the chaise, I get to work.

If there's one thing about how Mr. Sinclair runs things, it's that he keeps order. Nothing is ever out of place. We clean after each private show or event. He has cleaners come in every morning to clean the main floor. He does not do dirty or grungy like some strip joints. The day Mr. Sinclair took over for his grandfather was the day this place changed for the better. He is strict and if you step out of line, he calls you on it. Lord knows I've messed up a time or two. Not enough to lose my job, but I've had my ass handed to me.

One rule here at The Red Society, we do not use our real names. I go by Lettie at work. When I first started, I made the mistake of saying my name was Scarlett. Boy, did the boss let me have it. I was put on probation for ninety days for that. I get it though. I respect it. It's to keep the dancers safe. It's a way to protect us from pervs looking us up on social media. Not that anyone would find me anyway. I don't have time for social media. I lost all my friends at the age of sixteen. Not that I had many to begin with. My drunk mother scared any friends that I made off.

The day after my sixteenth birthday, my mother brought me here, paraded me into this club where she worked, and handed me over like I was fresh meat. I mean technically I was being underage and all. Mr. Sinclair's grandfather didn't care about those details. When he saw me, he saw dollar signs. What mother offers up her beautiful daughter with blonde hair and vibrant green eyes? Mine. I prayed hard that he wouldn't hire me. For whatever reason, the stars did not align, and I landed my first and well only job, as a dancer. That night, a part of me died. The old me was dead and in its place was a shell of a person dancing topless.

Just the thought of my early days here angers me. I was so young. I hated my mother for what she did. Some days I still do. But she is my mom and here I am.

I finish up and put the cleaner away before tossing the cloth into the wastebasket.

Sighing, I head for the dressing room to change into street clothes so I can go home. As soon as I walk in, I glance at the clock on the wall. It's not even ten thirty. Home before midnight? That's rare but I'll take it. I was up way late last night dealing with my mother's drunk aftermath. Beer bottles were everywhere. She was passed out hugging the toilet. I had to fetch her water and clean her up. I swear one day I'm afraid I'll arrive home and it will be too late to help her.

After changing, I walk to the intercom and press two. Someone from security will be up soon. Lucky for me, I don't have to wait long. In walks Vic almost immediately.

"Ready?"

"Yes."

Vic walks right beside me. Our arms practically touch. His dark skin pales mine significantly. He's good looking. Dark eyes, short dreads. Like all the other members of the security team, he's built. Taut muscles everywhere. I focus on the veins that nearly bulge out of his lower arm.

I glance at him, and he just looks at me and smiles. He's quiet. I like quiet. The less talking, the better in my opinion. When people talk, they usually want to know about you, your life, and that's the last thing I want to ever talk about. My life is far from a fairytale. There's nothing to discuss.

As soon as I am in my beater of a car, Vic smiles and

waves me off, standing there until I pull out. Yup. Security watches until the dancers turn onto the main road. As he fades into the darkness, my mind wanders back to Mr. Worthington. I shouldn't think about him. I never think of my clients. It's just there was something about him. I hope and pray the entire way home that I will not come home to a mess. I just want to shower and go to bed, hoping to dream of those green eyes.

Chapter Five

SPENCER

THIS IS LUDICROUS, me sitting out here. This isn't me. I'm not one to stalk. I wouldn't call this stalking, not exactly. That's what I tell myself anyway. I'm just making sure she gets to her car safely. That's all. It's not like I'm going to follow her to see where she lives. That would be stalking.

After last weekend, you'd think I would stay away from this place. But no, here I am parked in the dark. Shaking my head, I stare out and study the building.

Sitting back in my seat, I unbutton the top buttons of my dress shirt. It's nearly choking me. There is a camera that is planted directly above the back door. Another is mounted on the lamp post that sits in the middle of the parking lot where I assume only employees park.

I parked across the way in an adjacent lot so that no camera would pick up my vehicle. I don't need that damn owner coming out here questioning me about what the hell I am doing out here. The man oozes trouble and I don't dabble in that shit. I say that, yet here I sit.

About an hour passes before I see movement at the door. Security walks out first. I'll give the owner a little prop. He does make sure security detail is on point. He seems to actually care about his strippers. But that's about all I'll give the dude. He rubs me wrong. Maybe it's because Charla is fucking around with him now. She is stupid to do such a thing and honestly, I think she is only doing it to get her father off her ass. So far, it's not working.

The moment a certain blonde steps through the doorway, all thoughts of Charla fade away. Her head is cast down, hair hiding her face. She really shouldn't keep her head down. Regardless of whether security is out with her, she should check her surroundings.

I have a sudden urge to take over my knee to teach her a lesson in safety. My dick twitches under my dress pants. I bet she would let me too. Not many chicks I've been with like that kind of play, but I would bet a grand that she would let me do whatever I wanted. Just thinking about her letting me have my way has me fully erect now.

What the hell?

Now is not the time to think about Lettie like that. I adjust myself to try to relieve some of the pressure and continue watching her. She walks over to the shittiest car in the lot. It takes a bit for it to start.

That doesn't make sense. I know damn well she makes good money here. Why isn't she driving something nicer? Something more must be going on with her. Now I'm curious and want to know more.

I watch as she slowly pulls out. Security still stands out there, watching until she is on the main road, driving further away from the place.

Maybe I'll just follow her, just to see where she lives. I won't stop. I'll keep a safe distance. No, that's insane talk. I keep my eye on security until the back door shuts. The second it does, I pull out on the road before I can talk myself out of this stupid idea.

I speed down the road until I see her tail lights. Lettie is sitting at a red light. It's not hard to spot her car. It has seen better days. The blue paint is faded and chipped badly. When the light turns green, she hits the gas and smoke pours from the exhaust. It struggles to get up to speed, which causes me to lay off the gas. She really needs a better car.

Thoughts of wanting to bend her over again start to creep into my mind and I have to force myself to think of other things, like driving too close to her. I ease off the gas again. It's not like she could tell it's me behind her anyway. My tint is so dark it is illegal. I've received more than one ticket because of it. I don't give a fuck either. I walk right into the clerk's office, cash in hand, and slam it down on the counter. I've gotten friendly with the pretty brunette, whose name I don't know. Don't care to know. I just know she's a distraction when I need one. She sucks dick well and afterward, doesn't ask for more.

After driving for fifteen minutes, give or take, Lettie turns off onto a side street. Even though it's dark, I can tell this isn't the better part of town. Some of the streetlights are burnt out and the ones that aren't cast a sad glow on run-down houses, and overgrown lawns. She can't possibly live around here. I know she makes good money. I left a hefty tip when I rushed out and I know my private dance cost Charla a small chunk. The Red Society caters to the wealthy. No one walks in off the street. The average Joe couldn't afford the cover just to walk through those red doors. So, when the blonde dancer who has been stuck on my mind pulls into a shit hole apartment complex, I scratch my head. It only adds to the questions I have. When she kills the engine, I almost wonder if it'll ever start again. Can't worry about that right now though because she's already out of her car and retrieving something from the back seat.

Stupidly, I climb out of my car and quietly shut the door. I swear I'm not a fucking weirdo. I don't follow chicks like this. For some fucking reason I am drawn to her. Never once have I ever done something so reckless.

"Lettie," I call out, hoping this won't freak her out. The last thing I need or want is a restraining order for stalking.

Her body freezes immediately, but she doesn't turn toward my voice. I stay where I am, not wanting to scare her any more than I already have.

"It's Worthington." God, I do sound like a fucking stalker. Like some kind of crazed fan. Except I'm really not. I've never laid a hand on her. Not once. She might have turned me on to the point my hard dick was rubbing all over her barely covered pussy. Still, I never touched her.

She turns around, very slowly. Surprise is written across her face.

"Hey." I give a half wave.

So lame.

"Wha.. what are you doing here?"

Lettie looks around, like she's afraid someone will see

her talking to me. Fuck, she probably has a boyfriend or some shit. That never crossed my mind.

"I'm not sure exactly. I saw you leaving work and your car looked like it could leave you stranded any second, so I followed to make sure you made it home okay." I shrug. It's not a total lie.

The blonde pops a hand on her hip. "My car runs just fine. You should leave."

Putting my hands up in surrender, I need to play nice. I don't want her calling the cops. "Seriously, I was just concerned."

"Yeah, well guys like you have no idea what it's like in the real world. Go on, run back to your posh life." She turns and starts walking away.

Her smart mouth has me jogging up to her without thinking. I so badly want to punish her. Why? I'm still not sure.

"Now, that's not a way to treat a man who was concerned for your safety."

I gently grab her hand, stilling her. Her hand is ice cold. She turns, glaring at me for a moment.

"Fine, thank you for worrying about nothing. You are free to go now."

"You know that smart mouth of yours could get you into some trouble." I pull her close, and to my surprise, she lets me.

"What do you really want, Worthington?"

"Tell me something about you."

Lettie laughs a little and her green eyes soften a little. "I'm a stripper."

Damn this chick and her mouth. I feel my dick twitch

and will myself not to think about what it would be like to force her to her knees.

"Tell me something I don't know, Lettie."

She sighs, shaking her head. "I live here." She waves her free hand to the building behind us.

I nod. I didn't want to believe she could live here, however, her words just confirmed that she does in fact live in this shit hole. I don't like it. Not one bit. She should not be living here. Just standing out here gives me a bad vibe.

I slowly start to walk us back toward my black BMW. She doesn't fight me but I can tell she wants to question it.

"Sit in my car with me, just to talk."

Lettie stops dead in her tracks and eyes me. "You're not going to kill me, are you?"

"What?! God no. I know this looks creepy, but really we can go inside your place if you rather."

"Your car is fine. You have ten minutes then I really need to go."

"Deal."

Being the gentleman I was raised to be, I open the passenger door for her and close it the minute she climbs in. I have no idea what the hell I'm doing. I'm just winging it at this point. Very stupid of me considering I've never done something so damn stupid.

Once in, I turn the car on to run the air before turning to face Lettie. She looks nervous, her right knee is bouncing.

"Is it sex you want?"

Fuck, she is blunt. Straight to the point. I kind of like it. "No."

She nods as she processes my one word response. There's something about her. I can't quite put my finger on it. A familiar feeling maybe. The need to know her, and suddenly protect her. Hell, I don't really know. I'm not usually fucked up when it comes to women. I know what I want and there is no gray area.

"I don't usually follow women. There's just something about you."

"Oh."

We sit there in silence for a few minutes. I can barely see her face in the dark, but I can sure feel her eyes on me.

"Why did you rush out on me at The Red Society?"

It's the one question I really don't want to answer. Hell, I wouldn't even answer my best friend when she pried.

"You want the truth?"

"Yes."

Fuck it, might as well just come out and say it. "I left because had I not, I would have ended up bending you over that chair and fucking you senseless." I shrug my shoulders. That was pretty straightforward. I'm not the type to beat around.

Lettie opens her mouth but no words come out. I've shocked her, yet again. *Smooth, real smooth.*

She doesn't say anything, instead she leans over the console and grabs my fucking dick, stunning me silent. My cock was semi-hard before she grabbed it and now. Fuck.

"You're turned on." Her words are so matter of fact. I can practically hear the smirk in her voice.

"It would appear so."

"Is there something you want, Worthington?"

My breath catches as my dick twitches. There is no denying her feeling the movement either. She gives it a tighter squeeze, letting me know she felt it.

"I didn't come here wanting anything, but if you keep that up…" I don't finish that sentence. To afraid I'll fuck her right here and there's not a whole lot of room for the things I want to do to her.

"And now that you are here, is there something you want." Her sweet seductive voice just might be the death of me

"If you keep your hand on my dick, there might be."

"Is that so?" she questions as her fingers play with my zipper, slowly pulling it down. It's a slow form of torture. She's not really serious, is she? After all she doesn't know me from jack. I mean I won't deny her, but she has to be somewhat smart to not just fuck with a stranger. Right?

Who am I kidding? I fuck women who are strangers all the time. This would be no different, yet it feels different. I don't want her thinking I'm here for one thing.

After my zipper is down, she fumbles with the button. I place a hand over hers, stopping her for a minute.

"What are you doing?"

"You're not sure about this." She's not asking.

"I didn't say that."

I move her slender fingers and undo the bottom myself. I don't know how far this will go but I'm willing to go along for the ride. An unexpected ride.

I watch her hands that glow under the light from the dash touch me once again. Her fingers work like magic to free my erection. I have to suck in a breath when she strokes me once. Her touch is cold, yet it doesn't bother me.

"Lettie," I nearly hiss out when she starts stroking me slowly. It's pure agony.

"Worthington," she taunts.

It causes me to look up at her. I regret it almost instantly. The woman has nerves to lick her perfectly plump lips. She is teasing me.

I will be punishing her.

Tonight.

Chapter Six

SPENCER

G RABBING the back of her neck, I pull her close to me. Close enough to feel her minty breath against my lips. I don't kiss her. No, instead I look her square in the eyes to try to gauge her reaction. Her eyes are filled with nothing but lust which is a bit of a surprise considering I'm a guy who just followed her back to her apartment.

"Such a smart mouth you have. I should put it to use."

"You want to punish me?" Her voice is innocent. Her eyes, though, they tell a different story.

"Yes," is all I manage to choke out while resisting the urge to pull her by her blonde hair to my lap.

"Okay." Lettie winks.

Fucking hell.

My composure snaps. I force her face down to where my hard cock awaits her mouth. Lettie doesn't even hesitate. Her hand grips me tightly as her mouth wraps around me.

This is not what I planned. Not at all.

But I'm sure as fuck going to take it.

She's aggressive. Sucking hard and gripping me even harder. I wrap my hand in her blonde hair, pulling it just enough to keep control. The way her mouth and tongue move, it's unlike any other blow job I have ever had.

I wish I could see her face. Unfortunately, this position makes that impossible. I want to see her. I want to watch her mouth take all of me. Just that vision alone has me losing control. I'm not going to last like this.

Lettie slows down, pausing at the tip of my head. Her hand continues a steady motion, sliding up and down my wet cock. It's enough to make my balls tighten.

I wonder if her brain has finally caught up with what she is doing. How reckless this really is. After all, I'm a damn stranger from the strip club she works at.

Suddenly, she deep throats me, over and over. I'm on the verge of shooting my cum down her throat. Is that what she wants? I don't know. Not sure I care at the moment.

My orgasm surges through me, jutting into her mouth. Her head bobs up and down all the while my hand is still fisted in her hair, not allowing her to come up. I want her to suck up every last drop of my cum.

She takes it like a champ.

Lettie milks my cock dry like her life fucking depends on it. Like she craves the taste of me.

My breathing is still rapid when I release her hair. Slowly, she pulls back and looks at me. Her dark makeup is a mess. She swipes her thumb across her bottom lip before licking it. My dick jumps, wanting more.

She doesn't say anything. Instead she reaches for the door. She's leaving. I should just let her go. I got more than

I wanted. I should be satisfied, but for some stupid reason, I don't want her to go just yet.

"Wait."

Lettie turns to me with a questioning look. "What?"

"Where are you going?"

She hooks a thumb over her shoulder. "Um, home?"

I take a look at her attire, thinking of ways I can repay her. I could punish her a little more. She's in a pair of sweats. I can easily pull them down.

"Pull your pants down."

"I don't think so. It's not necessary that you get me off too."

"Yes, it is. Do as I say."

"Is this another punishment?"

I think about her question. Does she get off on being punished? I bet she does. I bet she likes it like hard.

"Yes. Now pull your pants down."

Heat glimmers in her eyes as she does as she is told. She's bare. Reaching over, I let my fingers lightly touch her. So soft and smooth.

"Use the lever, lean your seat back. Keep your hands up by the head rest."

I want a better view, and better access. I also don't want her touching me too much. Touching leads to distractions and feelings. That's not a road I want to go down. Not tonight.

Once the seat is back and her hands are in place, I slip a finger between her wet folds. Her breathing picks up in anticipation. I can hear wet she is. Sucking me off turned her on. Dirty, filthy girl.

The second my finger sinks into her pussy, she lets out a

quiet whimper. She's tight, and I wonder just how long it has been since she has fucked a guy.

Inserting a second finger, she nearly bucks forward in the seat. Pumping two fingers in and out, I let my thumb tease her clit. My plan is to just bring her to the brink of an orgasm and then stop. That will be her punishment. It's cruel and it will most likely make me an asshole, yet I bet she'll enjoy it to a degree. Something tells me she might like this game we are playing.

Lettie's hips buck more and more. I know she's getting close. Her one arm has slid down from the headrest and is now rubbing her breast over her clothes. I wonder what she looks like when she pleasures herself. That's a vision for another day because she's fucking close, I can feel her walls tightening. I stop moving my fingers.

Her green eyes shoot open. They are wild. "What? Why did you stop?"

I smirk in response, running a finger between her folds, careful not to touch her clit.

"Worthington?"

Lettie's voice is desperate. She wants a release. One I don't plan to give. I pull my finger back and bring it to my mouth, sucking on it.

"Fuck! Fine, I'll do it myself."

In one quick move, she lifts her top, ripping her bra down, exposing her tit. She takes the hardened nipple between two fingers. Her other hand reaches down between her legs.

Well damn. She is fucking touching herself in my car.

Within seconds, she's moaning out. I can't help but

grip my semi hard dick as I continue watching her roll her pebbled nipple between her fingers.

Mesmerized I watch as she comes undone on my leather seat. Her moans fill my car. I watch as she finally pulls her hand back, fingers covered in her juices. It's the hottest thing I've ever witnessed.

Without thinking, I snatch her hand, bringing her fingers to my mouth. Her eyes snap open as she watches me suck her clean. She glares at me, letting me know she is mad.

I don't care and I know it's beyond stupid, but I want to sink into her pussy, fucking her until the sun comes up.

Hollering from outside snaps us out of our private little bubble. I glance out of my windshield which is partially steamed up.

The hollering grows louder, clearer. Someone is shouting for someone named Scarlett. A woman, who seems to be stumbling around. Without giving it a second thought, I look back at Lettie, anxious to see where else this goes. However, when her eyes meet mine, I'm met with fear.

Her eyes now wide are the very opposite of wanting me. She quickly pulls her pants up and fixes her shirt quickly.

"I have to go." Lettie sounds almost panicked.

"Is everything okay?"

"No, yes, I just, I have to go. It was nice seeing you again."

Before I can say anything else, she's out of the car, slamming the door.

I lean up, watching through the glass and she rushes up to the woman who was yelling. Lettie seems to be trying to calm her down, but the woman doesn't seem to be having it. Then in slow motion, I watch as the woman slaps Lettie across the face before stumbling away.

What in the hell? I go to step out of the car, but Lettie rushes after her, disappearing into one of the apartments.

That woman was calling for Scarlett.

What does Lettie—

It hits me. Lettie is not her real name.

Chapter Seven

SCARLETT

"I KNEW I heard your car. What took you so long?" my mother calls out while looking past me to the vehicle I just exited.

I silently cringe, unable to look back as my feet continue to move forward. My cheeks feel hot. I can't look back at his flashy black car. The one I just got out of.

Mr. Worthington followed me. That fact alone is both scary yet thrilling. Was he inside the club watching me earlier?

"Scarlett?"

My mother stops and slaps me. I wasn't expecting it either. This is what I get in return for a little me time. I get fucking slapped.

If my cheeks weren't red before, they certainly are now. She's drunk. Her glossy eyes give her away, but she's not plastered.

Yet.

"What were you doing getting out of that fancy car?"

I step around her, and remind myself not to roll my

eyes. Just that gesture alone could set her off and since there's no telling just how much she's had to drink, I don't dare, not after I was just slapped across the face.

"That was just a friend. I was having trouble starting my car, so they followed me to make sure I made it home okay." The lie rolls off my tongue easily.

I learned to lie to my mother years ago, when I first caught on to her drinking habits. I used to hate having to lie to her, but it's better this way.

"That was sweet. Did you make decent money tonight?" I hate how quickly she changes her tone. Like she actually cares. She acts like she didn't just slap me outside of our apartment.

I let out a sigh. Every night that I work, I am asked this question. The only exception is on nights that she is already passed out from alcohol consumption.

"I did okay," I say as I continue toward my room.

Before shutting the door behind me, I hear my mother's words from the living room. "I bet if you lost a few pounds, you'd make more money."

I grind my teeth together to keep from saying something that will start a war. It's not worth it with her, even though it pisses me off to no end.

Quietly shutting the door and locking it, I strip out of my clothes and make my way to the bathroom. When we moved in here, I demanded the master. My mom tried to argue me on it, but it was the one time I held my ground. I am the one working to pay for this place. I deserve it.

I turn the water to the hottest setting. I am still wound up. Worthington had me suck his cock, no questions asked. I know it was a form of punishment. One I happened to enjoy. I'm not sure why it excited me as much as it did. I've never had a stranger follow me home, have me get in his car, and do unspeakable things.

The one thing I do know is I want to do it again.

Shaking my head to clear the wild thoughts, I step under the weak spray of water. It's hot, but not as hot as I would like. I probably have eight minutes tops to shower before the water turns cold.

As I rush to wash myself, I can't help but picture beautiful green eyes. His firm hand grabbing the back of my neck and pulling me down to his thick cock. How he wouldn't let me come. I was so desperate I did it myself. Then in a split second our private moment was over, thanks to my mother.

I turn off the shower and wonder if I will ever catch a break from this nightmare that is my life. As I go to wrap the towel around me, I hear my mother pounding on my door. "Scarlett dear, I need more money."

"For what? Rent is due in three days."

"So, work a little harder tomorrow to earn rent. A hundred should be enough for me."

I bite my tongue. Hard. Even as the metallic taste fills my mouth, I don't let up for fear I might scream out at the woman who birthed me. I fear I would tell her what's really on my mind and that would be to fuck off. She's not getting a dime. However, that will only start problems. The fact that I don't know how much she has had to drink is an issue. If she has had too many, shit gets ugly, throwing, breaking dishes. Dishes that I really can't afford to replace even with going to the local thrift stores.

Which is truly pathetic, Scarlett.

I make good money. It's enough to cover the bills and maybe then some. If only I wasn't handing my drunk mother money weekly, sometimes daily to feed her bullshit habit.

God, I need to stop. I tell myself this often. Stop enabling her. Stop putting up with it. Stop living like this. But how? The guilt creeps in every time and I end up caving.

My mother raised me alone. Single from the day I was born until I was sixteen. It was hard for her. She struggled to keep clothes on my back as a growing child. I never had fancy lunchboxes and cool accessories. She did the best she could. At least I'd like to think she did. I can't recall if she was sober back then. She was nice most of the time or tired from being overworked. If she was drunk, I was too young to realize it.

Climbing into bed, I close my eyes and wish for better days. Better days where a real man, maybe one like Worthington, values me. I wish for better days where I'm not just a stripper supporting her drunk mom.

But most of all at this very moment as I begin to drift, I want nothing more than to be back in the expensive vehicle, the feel of leather beneath me and his hands on my body.

I'm PUTTING on the finishing touches of my bubble gum pink lipstick when the intercom beeps followed by Mr. Sinclair's voice.

"Lettie, can I please see you in my office?"

I freeze. Shit. Did he see Worthington follow me? Am I

in trouble? Slowly, I get up from my dressing table and walk over to the intercom.

"Yes, sir, I'll be right up."

A few of the girls turn and look at me. I just shrug my shoulders and walk out. What's there to say? I don't know why the boss wants to see me. I may have an idea and I fear if it is correct, I'll be out of a job.

I knock slowly. "Sir, you wanted to see me?"

"Come in,"

I cast my eyes down, my red corset gives me something to focus on, that and the mesh panties I'm currently wearing. I hope I'm not being fired. Please. I need this job. I stop in front of his desk, unsure if I should sit.

"Have a seat."

I do as I'm told and finally brave a look at my boss. He is the one man who intimidates me. Not in a scary kind of way, it's just he holds all the cards to my life in his hands and he knows it.

Mr. Sinclair nods to the papers in front of me on the desk. My eyes go wide as relief floods me. A contract. He wants something from me. This I can do.

"Oh of course, sir," I say to him as I lift the pen, flip through pages to the last one, and sign away.

Yes, I've done this before. No, I'm not ashamed. Sexual favors I can do. The contract I just signed is for both of us. To protect us both. It's purely consensual. Yes, I realize this looks like prostitution and maybe to some degree it is. However, I could use an escape. Bonus, I'm not being fired. And the pay, well the pay alone is worth it. It's more than a week's worth on the dance floor. We both get something of pleasure out of it. I'll gladly take it.

The second I finish signing, Mr. Sinclair scoots his chair back. His thick cock is already out and ready for me. I nod, licking my lips. I know what the boss wants.

Getting up, I walk around his massive desk and drop to my knees in front of him while grabbing him.

Very slowly, I drag my tongue from his base to his head, licking the precum that has pooled there. His cock jumps as I take all of him. My rapid movements cause my eyes to water. Each time he hits the back of my throat, they water more. This will surely mess up my makeup. I don't care though. My hand grips him tighter as I continue sucking.

East grabs the back of my hair, forcing me to suck faster. He must be getting close. He's always rough when he's close.

I vaguely hear the sound of a door opening. I almost want to stop, to see who is on the other side, but I don't. Mr. Sinclair did not advise me to stop.

"Charla?"

"Oh my god! I... I need to leave."

"Shut the door, Charla."

Who is Charla? I wonder while my mouth is still wrapped around Mr. Sinclair's dick.

"I said shut the door."

Suddenly, Mr. Sinclair slides the chair back causing his cock to fall from my mouth. My spit covers him as he gets up and walks past the woman, slamming the door shut. He has no shame.

"How did you get past security?"

"Um, that's a complicated story." The woman has blonde hair, beautiful blonde hair. She doesn't work here. That much I know.

44

"I want to hear it," Mr. Sinclair simply states as he grabs himself.

I wonder if I should stay here on my knees or quietly excuse myself. This has never happened during one of our agreements before so I'm not quite sure what to do.

Mr. Sinclair speaks again, startling me. "I want to hear your complicated story."

The blonde looks nervous. I'd be nervous too. A hot man with a lip ring standing in front of her with a raging hard on.

"Well, I came in and asked the guy at the bar where I could find you. He ignored me and so I went to leave, realizing coming here was a bad idea."

"It was, go on."

"As I was heading for the door some large man asked me what the hell I was doing and that you requested me. He pointed to your door and told me to get moving before I pissed you off. So here I am."

Man, someone is going to be in trouble for letting a random woman walk through the club. They will probably be fired. Glad I'm not that person today.

Mr. Sinclair grabs the woman by her wrists. Is he? No. Yes, he is bringing her toward me. I feel heat creeping up my face. I watch on as he grabs the chair and positions it exactly how he wants. Then he sits the woman right down in it like she's going to watch us. He can't be serious.

He makes his way back to me, nodding as he strokes himself once. He wants me to continue. Well shit. This is new. Now I won't lie, I've done some things with Sinclair and other men, but there's never been another woman around. I take him back into my mouth without making eye contact with the woman. I'm not sure I want to see her reaction.

"I think I should go."

"You will do no such thing," Mr. Sinclair all but growls. "You will watch. I want your eyes on us the entire time."

Damn, that is kind of hot. My body heats with desire as I continuing sucking his cock.

"East," the woman quietly calls out. East Sinclair. I've never called him by his first name. It's always sir, Mr. Sinclair, or boss.

"You heard what I said," he states firmly and then grips my hair, making me suck faster, harder. Tears fall from my face faster now as he makes me take him deep, hitting the back of my throat. Wetness pools between my legs. I don't know why, but him being forceful turns me on at an entirely different level.

"Fuck, Scarlett." Mr. Sinclair uses my real name as he thrusts hard. Hot cum spills into my mouth. I swallow as I continue sucking, making sure to get every last drop of him. When I release him, he immediately helps me to stand. He then reaches for a tissue and wipes my face. He has always been good at cleaning up. As soon as he finishes, he turns me around to face his desk.

"Bend over, Scarlett, your turn."

"That's it! I can't take anymore." The woman stands from the chair in a rush. Mr. Sinclair walks straight to her.

"You barge into my office, you will sit your perfect little ass back down." I can't help but notice my boss's dick is still rock hard.

In one swift motion, the woman slaps him. Hard. My mouth falls open at the sound. I watch in shock as the woman storms out of the office, slamming the door behind her. Wow.

Mr. Sinclair turns back to me, "Good girl, you'll be rewarded now." He walks over to me like he wasn't just slapped across the face. The red mark is the only proof that it in fact happened.

I smile as he pulls open a drawer. My thighs squeeze shut, knowing what's coming. This type of play takes me to different heights. It allows me to escape to the highest mountain and I cannot fucking wait.

Mr. Sinclair pulls out a bottle of lube and a silver plug. He sets them on the desk. He brings his hand around and dips two fingers into me. I'm soaked.

He continues pumping his fingers into me while his other hand takes the lube and pours it between my cheeks. I tense as soon as he removes his fingers and brings them to my hole. He inserts one finger and then another, slowly stretching me. I can't help but grind against his desk. I need more, want more.

The second he removes his fingers, I know the plug will be inserted. Just the thought thrills me. He takes the plug and runs it along my ass. It's cool as it glides against me. I pop my ass out and wait. I'm growing impatient.

"Sir, please."

"Please what?"

I respond by moving my ass. He knows what I want.

He slaps my ass hard, causing me to yelp. "Sir, please give it to me."

Mr. Sinclair sighs as he finally inserts the plug. Instantly, I tighten around it.

"Yes, sir, yes," I can't help but call out. I am wound so

fucking tight that it's pure hell to wait to see what he decides to do with my pussy.

I hear the vibration before I see it. Turning my head, he pulled out a blue vibrator. I can't remember if we have used this one before. Don't care either, as long as he uses it.

The minute he thrusts it into my pussy, I grind against his desk in desperate need. Pure fucking ecstasy is what this is. I climb that mountain of pleasure so fast that I know my hips will have bruises from how hard they continue to hit his desk. It's worth it though.

Within minutes I have reached the top. I don't look back as I jump, chasing my orgasm back to the bottom.

Then we do it all over again.

Chapter Eight

I CAN'T GET a certain blonde out of my head, that's a dilemma. So much shit has gone down since I last saw Lettie, or should I say Scarlett? I'd like to ask her about her name, except I don't have her number and I'm almost certain that Lettie is a stage name so really there is no reason to ask.

But I want to.

That's not my only problem though. Charla and East have created some issues. Yeah, my best friend is fucking around with the owner of the club where Lettie happens to work. Talk about making things complicated.

The dude may have helped Charla dodge Corey and his bullshit, but I don't like the two of them together. I'll admit that East is a better man than Corey and treats his employees good. I still don't like him. Don't like seeing Charla and him together.

As much as I'd like to sit and dwell on their situation, I can't. There's someone else I would rather focus my time on.

Her.

She has plagued my mind like no other. I can't figure it out. No chick has ever captured my attention long enough. Not even close. I don't know what it is about her. I can't put my finger on it and it's driving me nuts.

I guess that's why I am once again sitting in my car waiting for her. The only difference is, this time I'm parked at her apartment complex.

Now that I know where she lives, I can avoid the club and its cameras.

It is Thursday night, eight o'clock. I'm hoping she'll arrive soon. God, I sound like a damn lunatic. Not knowing Lettie's schedule makes this sort of hard. I don't know if she's at work or out doing whatever it is she does on her down time.

Part of me wants to leave and go find someone random to hook up with to take my mind off of Lettie. Yet for some fucking reason I can't make myself leave. I find Lettie interesting. Submissive almost. She willingly got into my car and followed my commands. My dick twitches remembering.

Fuck, I hope she pulls in—

I hear the sound of her exhaust before I even see the car. She really needs a new one. That's something else that has been on my mind. She works at a high-end strip club yet lives in this dump of an apartment complex and drives that thing.

I'm out of my car and walking toward hers before she has even got the thing in park. As she shuts it off smoke blows out from the rear. Yeah, we'll be discussing that.

"Lettie," I call as I reach her car.

Her hand flies to her chest. "Jesus!"

I smirk knowing I startled her. My smile drops as I realize she wasn't paying attention to her surroundings yet again. She needs to be more careful, especially here. Now I want to punish her for being so reckless.

"What are you doing here, Worthington?"

"Spencer." I pause giving her a moment to process my name. "Is my first name, and I came to see you."

"Oh."

I've caught her off guard. She was not expecting that. I take her in from head to toe.

Lettie's blond hair is pulled back. She's in gray cotton shorts and a tight fitting tank top. The top of her breasts nearly spill out of it. East shouldn't let his dancers leave half naked. They should be fully covered when they walk out that back door. Unless she wasn't coming from work. Nope, don't want to think about that.

"Why did you come to see me?"

Her question snaps me back to the present. Why did I come again? To see if she'll let me take control again.

"Uh, Spencer?"

Fuck! The way my name rolls off her tongue. I kind of like it. My dick likes it too.

"Let's go grab something to eat."

Lettie looks at me with a puzzled look. "You want to take me out to grab food?" She points to herself like what I've just said doesn't make any sense.

"That's what I said."

She laughs, shaking her head. "Get out of here, I'm not part of your class of people." She turns and starts walking away.

"Lettie." I keep my voice firm. "I didn't ask. Now go change so we can go grab something to eat."

She freezes, not bothering to turn around. "You might want to get my name correct if you are going to start making demands that I go somewhere with you." When the last word leaves her mouth, she turns to face me with a smart ass look across her face.

The need to punish her grows as my dick strains against my slacks. Little does she know that I caught her name and that she is in for a rude awakening.

"Fine, *Scarlett*, go change now. I won't tell you again."

The shit eating grin that was plastered on her face seconds before falls. I have her right where I want her.

"Go, now. Before I decide to skip food and punish your smart mouth instead."

Lettie nods, moving quickly toward her unit. She doesn't say a single thing and I begin to think that maybe I have crossed a line and scared her. That is until she reaches her door and turns around to look me dead in the eyes.

"Maybe I like being punished."

Fuck me.

And then I wait.

And wait.

Twenty minutes have passed. I'm fucking pacing outside of her door like a weirdo. There is no noise coming from the other side. None that I can hear anyway. What the hell is taking so long? I said change, not shower, and throw on a bunch of girly shit.

I'm about ready to pound on the door to find out what the fuck is taking so long when she suddenly rushes through the door. Lettie looks visibly upset.

"What is wrong?"

She rushes by me, grabbing my hand as she goes. She is in a rush to get away from her place.

"Wait a minute, Lettie. What— "

"My name is Scarlett! Stop calling me by my stage name."

I put my hands up in surrender. "Woah, okay. What the fuck is going on?"

It dawns on me the closer we get to my car, maybe she has someone, a boyfriend, girlfriend. Hell, she could be married. I'm not looking for that sort of trouble. I don't need that kind of shit in my life. I may fuck women and nothing more, but I don't mess around with woman who have attachments.

"Do you have a boyfriend, or someone I should know about?"

She turns and glares at me, her breathing is heavy. "What? God no. Who dates a stripper?"

I shake my head as I open the passenger door to allow Scarlett to get in. Before she slides in, I grab her wrist, stilling her.

"That is just a job, Scarlett. You still have a life outside of that club."

"You wouldn't know anything about my job other than being there for a good time." She snatches her hand away and gets in.

Shutting her door, I walk to my side of my black BMW, digesting what she just said. She is right, I don't really know anything about her job. However, I'm sure she must have some life outside those red doors. One that might not be the best based on where she lives and how urgent she is looking to get out of here.

Before climbing in, I glance at her unit. The dingy blinds are split, someone is peeking through them, watching us. The question is who?

Scarlett is hiding something. She is a mystery, one I want to find out more about.

SCARLETT

SPENCER PULLS UP to this expensive looking restaurant in the downtown area. I never come here. Can't afford it, never could. Just the thought of walking into that place makes my skin crawl. For one, I am not dressed in proper attire. I'm wearing the nicest thing I own. I'm wearing a pair of black skinny jeans that I paired with a yellow top and black heels that have way too many scuff marks on them. I call it my looking for a job attire. Whenever I think I can look for a real job, I put this on and head out. My mother laughs every time I return with not one application. Just thinking about that reminds me that this, being here with Spencer, is a bad idea.

"What's wrong?" Spencer asks from the driver seat.

I turn to face him. Concern is etched across his face. I am way out of his league. It is almost embarrassing. We do not make sense. None of this does.

"Why do you want to take me out?"

He tilts his head, debating. I can tell. I've seen it all

before on men. My stupid heart sinks thinking about how stupid I am. I can feel my face heat.

"I am taking you out because I want to. I'd like to get to know you. Is that okay?"

"Oh."

I'm not sure what else to say so I wring my hands together in my lap while replaying what he just said to me. I'm not sure I should believe him. I mean any smart girl wouldn't, right?

"Stop that," he says as he puts his hands over mine. "Can't I just take you to dinner?"

"Okay, let's go to dinner." I nod before I can change my mind. I can't believe I'm letting some rich stranger take me out.

Spencer gets outs and rounds his car as I'm opening my door. He holds his hand out for me to take. This is a first. It feels foreign, placing my hand in his. His hand is so much larger than mine and I'm not really use to the idea of hand-holding.

We walk into The Vine. It's not a very large restaurant but smells absolutely amazing. I don't think I have ever smelled food this good, which is pretty damn pathetic when I think about it. That's my reality. Another slap in the face as to why I should not be mixing with such a man. Spencer is way out of my league.

The atmosphere is dark. The walls are black with gold accents, frames, paintings. There's lights strung through-out. The kind that you might find in fancy backyards during summer time. That's something I've only seen in magazines while waiting to check out at the grocery store.

I stand behind Spencer as he speaks to the hostess. I

hope my outfit is okay here. He is dressed casually but makes it look so good. Khaki pants and a solid blue polo. He fits in here. I do not. He glances at me, smiles, and tugs my hand, bringing me to stand next to him. The gesture makes me feel special.

Almost.

I catch the hostess giving me a disgusted look. She recovers quickly and offers me a fake smile. Her bright teeth are blinding. I don't bother to return the smile. I know my place. It's not here.

"Excuse me, do you have an issue?" Spencer's words shock me. My eyes fly to his face. He is looking directly at that bitch of a hostess. He must have caught the look she gave me because he is pissed.

The hostess shakes her head back and forth fast. "No, no sir."

"Good. I would hate for there to be an issue."

I can practically see the tears welling in the corner of her eyes. It makes me want to feel sorry for her. But I do not. Karma got her ass.

"Right this way, Mr. Worthington," the hostess says as she swings her fiery red hair that's been braided over her shoulder. Her hips sway as she leads us to our table. I can't help but resist him. I can't do this. I stay frozen in place.

"Scarlett?"

"I... I can't..."

Shaking my head, I don't bother finishing my sentence. . Spencer just stood up for me. No one besides my boss has ever had my back. Not a single person.

Spencer's green eyes stare back at me. The look he gives me has me putting one foot in front of the other. He smiles, looking relieved that I didn't put up a fight. I wanted to. Believe me, I wanted to. It's just there is something about this man that has me caving and doing whatever it is that he demands.

Spencer orders water which is odd to me. Don't all the rich kids order expensive drinks with names I can't pronounce? Me, I order a coke. Yup, so basic. Coke for me is a luxury. I can't afford to buy the stuff so when I do have it, it is a treat. I can't even remember the last time I had it. Again, pathetic.

We are both quiet as we look over the menu. Panic starts to set in. I've never ordered off of a menu like this before. The entrees are well... exquisite. I'm not even sure what some of it is. I feel my face flush with embarrassment over not knowing some of these terms.

"What's going through your mind?"

Shit.

"Nothing."

"Scarlett. Your face is red. What is it?"

I guess it's better to just come out and say it. Maybe the sooner I get this over with, the sooner he'll see that I'm not what he needs in his life.

"It's just, some of the stuff on this menu, I have no idea. I don't eat at places like this."

If Spencer was ashamed at my response, his face hides it well. His green eyes never leave mine. Not even when he goes to speak.

"Think of this as a new adventure. You're trying something new. Nothing wrong with that."

I smile, nodding. How does he make this sound so simple? He's charming. That should be a red flag.

"Tell me, what is it you like to eat? I can help with suggestions."

"Um, well simple. I don't eat anything fancy. You don't understand, I don't have the money to splurge on food. I buy simple, cheap."

I feel so foolish telling him this. I watch as he rubs his chin, digesting my words. I just told him something very personal, too personal.

"We're going to discuss why you don't have money, considering you work at the best club in the city. We won't discuss it now, but it will be discussed in the near future."

My mouth drops open and then closes. He wants to discuss my personal life with me. Does this mean he could possibly like me? No, no that is a wild idea. Another red flag. He's waving them in my face and yet I'm not running for the hills.

"Now Scarlett, let's start with the basics. Chicken, seafood, or steak?"

Chapter Ten

SCARLETT

"Uh, chicken." It has to be the safest choice. I don't think I've ever tried seafood. Maybe frozen fish sticks, but I'm pretty sure those don't count as seafood.

"There's Caesar salad with grilled chicken. Seared chicken breast with vegetables in a lemon garlic sauce, or there is chicken penne with asparagus."

I look over my options a few more minutes while trying to calm the anxiety I feel. Part of me says shit, try something new. The other part is screaming to run.

I don't run of course. Instead, I opt for the seared chicken breast with vegetables. It sounds like a safe option.

Once our order is in, I wait for the question that I know is coming. He wants to dig into my private life. I can't have that. I hardly know the guy. He's made of money. He'll never understand what it's like to walk in my shoes.

"How old are you, Scarlett?"

"Twenty-four. You?"

"Twenty-eight."

I nod. I can do simple questions. They are harmless.

"Have you always lived here?"

"I have, just outside of the city."

"Hmm." Spencer rubs he jaw in thought. "I've never seen you around. Not in school, or anything. I would have remembered you."

I laugh. "I hardly think we would have ran in the same circle and most definitely not the same school. I'm sure you went to some prestigious private school."

"I did go to a private school. Don't be so quick to judge. I may have money and look like a pretty boy to you, but I'm not some rich asshole. At least not most of the time."

"But you are some of the time?" I say, raising an eyebrow, smiling.

The banter between us is light and fun. Something I have not experienced since my high school years, and those were short lived. Kind of hard to go to school when you dance all night and sleep most of the day. I had to drop out and enroll for my GED. College, yeah right. Not on my radar.

"So, tell me about your financial issues. I know you make good money. What is going on?"

My smile fades as the last word leaves his mouth. So much for light talk.

"I take care of my mother. She's not able to work."

It's as simple as that. He does not need to know the details. Doesn't need to know that my mother's alcohol addiction drains me.

"Is she sick?" he asks.

I nod, taking a sip of my Coke so I don't have to speak

the lie. I guess you could say she is technically sick. She has an addiction.

"That has to be hard."

"You have no idea."

I want to say more, to tell him that he has never had to worry a day in his life about paying rent or the electric bill. That he has never had to strip to make money. Luckily for both of us, our food arrives and we eat in silence.

THE DRIVE back to my place is quiet. I'm not sure what to expect once we get back. Spencer has been a gentleman all night. Will he expect me to invite him in? Because that will be a hard no. He cannot see what is beyond the outside of my apartment. Never.

The minute we pull in, my nerves kick in, I start chewing my lip trying to think of ways out of whatever scenario he might throw my way.

"I enjoyed tonight," Spencer says as he puts his car in park.

"I did too. Thank you for dinner. It was delicious."

Spencer smiles, leans toward me, and puts his arm around my shoulder, pulling me in close. My heartbeat begins to race as I anticipate what comes next. Kissing. I haven't kissed in well.. I don't know.

"You smell amazing," he whispers into my neck. Thoughts of when I was last kissed are forgotten as he moves down to my collarbone, leaving a little trail of heat behind as he nips at my skin.

I'm left feeling cold the second Spencer removes his lips

and pulls back. He looks at me, the desire evident in his emerald eyes. It makes me both excited and scared. How far will this go? Thinking about sex is embarrassing only because it has been way too long since I have actually had sex. I was just with Mr. Sinclair, but that was not sex. That was us pleasuring each other without actual sex. That's how I like it. No strings attached. No feelings.

"Scarlett?"

I shake my head. Shit, was he talking to me? "I'm sorry, I was lost in thought."

"Hot and bothered already?" He laughs. "Imagine what would happen if I were to touch you, and put my mouth here?" His hand slides to my lap where he rubs his hand over my jeans.

"Spencer," I whisper.

"Scarlett?"

My mind is reeling. Part of me wants him to touch me, yet another part of me asks why he wants to. That part wins.

"What's in this for you?" I'm blunt and to the point.

"What's in it for me?"

I stare at the gorgeous man in front of me. I want to see his response, to be able to read his face when he answers. This might be all fun and games for him and that's fine, but I don't really have time for that nonsense. Not that I really have time for anything serious either. Either way, it will most likely end horribly.

"I saw a beautiful girl dancing. I decided I wanted to get to know her a little better. Where this will go, I am not entirely sure. I'll be honest, I don't typically do relationships. However, there is something about you that I like. Is that okay?"

Spencer's face gives nothing away. He never even broke eye contact with me which leads me to believe he is at least being up front and honest. I'll take it.

"I guess it is, for now."

"You and your mouth. You also make me want to punish you in worst way."

His words have me squeezing my thighs. I think about the last time we were together and how he punished me.

"Like you did the last time we were in your car?"

He leans back in close to my ear. "Worse. So much worse." His hand leaves my lap as he runs it up my stomach to my breasts. He rubs a hand over them.

"The things I want to do to your body." He breathes into my ear as he pulls my top and bra down. He pinches my nipple. Hard.

I cry out in pain. Pain that sends shockwaves straight to my pussy. It makes me want him to pinch me repeatedly. He doesn't though, instead he pulls his hand out and fixes my top.

"Soon, Scarlett. Soon."

Chapter Eleven

SPENCER

SOMEHOW I FOUND what little bit of restraint I had left and let Scarlett get out of my BMW. It wasn't easy. The way she writhes when I cup her pussy. Fuck. I wanted to drag her to the back seat and fuck her right then and there. There just isn't enough space back there for all the things I want to do to Scarlett's body. So I drove myself home with a raging hard on. One that I'm fixing to take care of as soon as the water warms up.

Charla texted me as soon as I walked in my door, asking me to come have a drink with her. I agreed, but first I need to let go of this pent up energy considering I haven't been with another woman since I started this thing, whatever it is, with Scarlett.

Stepping under the spray of water, I let it pour over me. Running my hands through my hair, I turn to allow the water to hit my back. Hoping it will ease some of my tight muscles. I ran this morning and took a quick shower at the gym before work but the water pressure at the gym is nothing like what I have here.

Enough about the gym, I tell myself as I grab my dick. I should have just fucked Scarlett in the back seat. Bet it would have been better than my hand. Just remembering how soaked she was when I fingered her has me stroking myself.

My gaze travels down. I watch what I'm doing to myself for a minute before closing my eyes. When I do, I picture Scarlett's pretty little mouth wrapped around my dick, sucking it. She sucked it so good too. My grip tightens on my dick. It causes me to lean forward, placing my free arm against the tiles as I keep pumping faster, harder.

My balls begin to grow tight as I continue picturing her bobbing up and down on my dick, deep-throating it. How it felt fucking fantastic when I came down her throat.

At that thought, my muscles start to contract and I lose control as hot cum shoots out all over the shower floor. I continue bracing myself until my dick stops jerking and my heart rate begins to settle.

I relax back into the water to wash myself. The hot water pounding on my back is soothing

Once I've finished washing my body, I cut the water and grab a towel, wrapping it around my waist. There's another text from Charla, asking where I'm at. Damn, she is impatient. She is lucky she is my best friend, otherwise I would ghost her needy ass.

Charla and I have been friends for what feels like our entire lives. We attended the same private school and ran in the same circle of friends. All wealthy. We never dated, instead we made a pack to always be friends no matter what life handed us.

I don't bother knocking as I unlock her door. Yes, I have a key. That's just how we do things.

"It's about time!" she calls out as she raises a glass of what I'm guessing is pink Moscato.

"I had to shower."

"And probably masturbate." Charla giggles, confirming she's had a bit to much to drink already. She would never openly talk about this, not while sober. She's too much of a prude in that sense. Must uphold her perfect image.

"Sure did, it felt good too," I reply, grabbing my dick as I walk up to her.

"Ew, Spence! I don't need to know these things. Grab a glass."

"You brought it up."

I grab a stemless glass and hold it out for Charla to pour the wine into it. For the record, I only drink wine with her.

"So, what's the special occasion?"

"Oh, you know, just my father demanding I marry Corey."

I nearly spit my wine back into the glass. "Excuse me? That's a new low. Even for Stefan."

Stefan has always been hard on Charla. Always expected her to be perfect, still expects too much. He groomed her into this perfect daughter and now she doesn't know how to tell him no. She doesn't know how to stand up for herself. It pisses me off because Corey is a complete douche bag and Charla deserves way better.

"Yes, but I think I got East to agree to fake date me, so that should getting him off my back. At least I hope it will."

"What?!"

Fuck! If I wasn't angry over her father's bullshit, now

I'm really angry. There's something about East that I just don't like. I don't want her dating him, even if it is a front to get her dad off her back.

"Chill, Spence, it's not a big deal."

"I don't like the dude."

I watch Charla take a sip of her wine before setting it down on the white marble table in front of her. She whips her blonde hair behind her over her shoulder. The gesture makes me pause. I've seen my best friend brush her hair away hundreds of times. Never really paid attention, but there was something in the way she did it just now. Something that I can't put my finger on.

"Look, I know you don't care for him. I'm sure not many do, but I happen to enjoy him. He's nice to look at." She wiggles her eyebrows and starts laughing again.

"How much have you had to drink?"

"Not enough. I went to dinner with East earlier and Corey showed up with some bimbo on his arm. He made a scene at the restaurant."

I curse under my breath. "What the hell, Char? This has to stop. It's not healthy."

"You think I don't know that? That is why I'm hoping everything will settle down when my father sees me with East."

"I have a feeling it will only explode."

"You are probably right, but in the meantime, it'll be fun to be bad."

"Cheers to that," I say as I raise my glass.

Maybe Charla will find her voice after all.

❧

I wake suddenly to commotion. My head pounds slightly. Why? I sit up and rub my eyes. I'm in Charla's guest room. Right. Last night. Too much wine.

Hell.

I plop back down hoping to shut it all out, but the commotion grows louder. It's like people are shouting.

I sit up and listen. I can't quite make out what the voices are saying. Getting up, I grab the shirt I threw on the chair, and pull it over my head. Very slowly I open the door and just listen.

"Charla Ann! What has gotten into you?"

Stefan. Her father is here. Great. I listen more, unsure if I should make my presence known, or if I should just stay in here and pretend I'm still sleeping.

"Daddy, Corey has put bruises on me. He's tried to force himself on me. I won't have it and you shouldn't want that for me."

"Don't be silly. He told me about your arm."

"He did?" Charla asks, confusion laced in her voice.

"Of course. What else was he supposed to do to prevent you from being with that punk?"

"That's not what happened! Seriously, that's what Corey told you?"

Charla's angry, rightfully so. Corey is a lying fuck. There's been numerous times I've wanted to lay the fucker out, but Stefan holds a lot of control. I have a good business and I wouldn't put it past him to try to bury me should I hit his damn puppet.

I'm angry for Charla. Why won't her father listen? Stepping into the hallway I pause once more.

"Calm down, Corey would not lie to me."

"Oh, but he did because Corey was in my face fighting with me and grabbed me to prevent me from leaving him. Mr. Sinclair, or should I say the punk, happened to be walking past and saw the entire thing."

"Now Charla." Laughter leaves Stefan's lips.

"No, Daddy! Don't Charla me. Corey was hurting me. This has happened more than once. I'm done. Do you hear me?"

There's a moment of silence, I almost wonder if Stefan finally sees, maybe he's consoling her. I wait.

"Perhaps if Corey kept his nasty hands off of me, I wouldn't be seeing East now."

Oh hell, Charla. Fuck. I wouldn't have thrown that out there. She's going to need backup. Slowly I start to walk down the hall toward their voices. I will the pain behind my eyes to ease.

"Don't be ridiculous, you are not seeing that man. That stops today."

"I am and I will continue seeing him. There's nothing you can do to stop that. How about you believe your own daughter for once?"

I continue walking until I'm just inside the living room. Both turn my way. Two sets of eyes staring. One filled with rage, the other filled with desperation.

"Spencer." Stefan nods my way.

"Sir." I swallow. "What Charla is saying is true. Corey has pushed himself on her more than once." I'm hoping my statement will help him see the truth.

"Enough, Spencer. This conversation is between Charla and I. You should show yourself out."

Charla's mouth gapes as she looks at me with a defeated look. I nod once. There is no getting through to her father.

"I'll call you later, Charla. Mr. Krauss, for what it's worth, Mr. Sinclair has been nothing but a gentleman to your daughter. He treats her better than Corey ever has. Ever will."

With that, I walk past the two of them and head for my place. I hope whatever war is brewing, Charla comes out in one piece.

My phone goes off the minute I shut the door to my place. The sun shines a little too brightly through the floor-to-ceiling windows. From beyond is the ocean.

Pulling my phone out of my back pocket, I see that it's Charla.

Come back

I sigh, her father must have left. She would never pull out her phone in the middle of a heated conversation with her father. Never. I decide to brush my teeth and throw on deodorant before heading back down to her floor. It's nice living in the same condominium as Charla. She's on the seventh floor while I reside on the top and tenth floor. There are only a few other suites on this floor due to the size of our condos. I like it that way. Less nosey neighbors.

Ten minutes later, I'm unlocking Charla's door. Again. When I step inside though, it's quiet.

"Charla?"

Silence. I pull my phone out to make sure I didn't misread her text. Two words are on the screen. Kind of hard to mess that up. I decide to head for her room, maybe she's thrown herself into bed after dealing with her father.

The door is cracked, so I slowly push it open. She's not in bed, but I hear water running. I take a few steps toward the bathroom door that is wide open and pause. This is uncharted territory. I've never seen Charla naked. A skimpy two-piece sure. Barely there lounge clothes, yup. But fully naked and standing under a spray of water, no.

I take a slow step in, unsure of what to do. Maybe the glass will be fogged over. When I brave a glance toward her shower, I'm surprised by the sight on the other side of the glass. There stands Charla under the spray of water, fully clothed.

I peek around the glass to get a look at her. "Charla, are you okay?"

The only response I get is a slight nod. She looks like she's on the verge of breaking down. It kills me. I do the only thing I know to do at this moment. I pull Charla out from under the water and embrace her. She's soaked to the bone, but I don't care.

It takes my best friend all of five seconds before she breaks down crying. She finally lets go of all she's been holding back and loses it right there completely soaked in my arms.

Chapter Twelve

SCARLETT

I HAVEN'T SEEN Spencer in over a week. We've both been too busy. I work extremely late some nights. He works late too and seems exhausted by the time he leaves. I get it. Work drains the life out of you. I thought I was the only one that happened too, but I guess not.

Spencer did invite me out to some fancy event. I declined. There's no way I could attend such a thing. I don't even own a nice dress let alone some sort of gown. Just thinking about going and being around such people. People full of wealth and expensive shit. No thanks.

More proof that our two worlds should not collide. We live different lives. Whatever this is will never flourish. We are bound to fall of the deep end and drown.

The minute I pull my car into my apartment complex, I spot it. My stupid heart skips a beat. The expensive black car parked where it usually is. I can't contain the smile on my lips as I get out of my car and head toward his. Spencer's tint is so dark. I wish I could see his face as I walk up to his car. The minute the passenger window rolls down though, I instantly take a step back. The man staring at me from the driver side is not Spencer.

"Hello, Scarlett." The man says my name as if he knows me. It startles me. I don't know him. I would surely remember his gorgeous face and perfect blonde hair.

"I'm sorry, I thought you were someone else." I start to back away, afraid to take my eyes off him. A million questions swirl through my mind. Does my mom owe him money? Did she steal from him? It wouldn't be the first time and if I had to guess it won't be the last. When I don't give into her needs, she usually finds another way to obtain the thing she loves the most.

"You don't have to go. We have much to talk about."

"I doubt that."

I can guarantee we have zero to talk about that would interest me in the least. Fuck, how can I be so stupid to walk up to a random car. I mean it's the same color, flashy, just like Spencer's.

"Believe me, Scarlett Ward, we do have lots to talk about. You need money. You're desperate for it. I think I can help you out."

How does he know I need money? That's a personal issue I don't share with people. I don't like it.

"Did Spencer send you here?" I blurt out. I can't help but ask. It annoys me to think that Spencer would send someone to help me with my financial situation.

The gorgeous man squints his brown eyes at me. He rubs his jaw, staying quiet for a moment. His silence annoys me further.

Raising an eyebrow, I snap, "Well?"

"No, Spencer did not send me. The fact that you know him is intriguing, but no, that's not why I am here."

So he knows Spencer, but that's not why he is here. Right. Like I believe this bullshit. I mean what are the actual chances of this stranger knowing Spencer but not coming here because of him? We come from different paths, there is no way this is random.

"I'm here to offer you some money. I just need to ask you a few questions."

"Are you a cop?"

"No. Come on, let's go for a ride and I'll explain everything."

"I am not going anywhere with you."

His phone rings, distracting him, and I take off for my apartment. I don't look back. Once inside I quickly lock the door even though I know it will do no good seeing as how cheap and weathered the door is. I hit the lights and wait a minute before peeking out of the thin blinds.

His car is still there, but the lights are now on, hopefully a sign that he's leaving.

"What on earth are you doing?"

Shit. I nearly have a heart attack as I jump back. For a moment I forgot about my mother. I let go of the blinds and turn to face her.

"Do you owe someone money again?"

"No." She pauses, clearly thinking. "At least I don't think I do."

Fucking hell.

"So there's a chance?"

My mother shrugs her shoulders before turning to head back toward the kitchen. I groan in frustration. Why? Why fucking me? I look out once more and see the black car is gone. Thank God.

I head to my bedroom without saying another word to my mother. Shit needs to change. I need to put my foot down. Or I need to leave her. I can do that.

Except I can't do that. I owe my life to her. She raised me alone and did the best she could with what resources she had. Even if it was a shit upbringing. I had no father in the picture. No child support to depend on. Just me and my mom. I love her. Deep down I really do. I just have grown to dislike the person she has become. I dislike the situation that she put us in. If only she could get her shit together and sober up. Yeah right. Hell would have to freeze over before that would ever happen.

Sighing because I can only see her as a loss cause, I crawl into bed, trying to push the nagging feeling of who that man was out of my mind.

I wake to my phone ringing. It never rings. Grabbing it, Spencer's name is on the screen. He never calls.

"Hello?" My voice is groggy.

"Hey, did I wake you?"

"Yes, no."

What time is it even? I pull the phone away to check the time. It is almost noon. Shit.

"Scarlett?"

"I'm here, sorry."

"Are you okay? It's nearly lunch time and you sound like you are sleeping."

"Yeah, it was a late night at work, and I had trouble sleeping."

It's not a total lie. I tossed and turned for quite a while

thinking about that man in the black car who knew my name. He knew too much. At some point sleep finally consumed me and now it is noon.

"Can I see you tonight, after the charity event?"

"I have to work."

"That's fine. I'm sure I will get out late as well."

"Okay."

"I'll text you later."

We end the call and I lay here, still completely tired like I got zero sleep. I listen, the place is quiet. Sometimes when the house is this quiet I wonder if my mother is still breathing. Sad, yet true. There has been plenty of occasions where I have stared at her chest to see if she was breathing or felt for a pulse.

God, I'm exhausted. So fucking exhausted.

Chapter Thirteen

SPENCER

I NEVER TEXTED Scarlett last night. I feel bad, but last night's charity event was a complete shit show and I had to stick around to do damage control.

Charla brought East which I thought was a terrible idea, even if I get why she did it. She's trying to prove to her father that She will not be with Corey. I give her props for sticking up for herself though.

I knew her father and Corey would be seated with us. That was a huge mistake too. The minute Corey put his hands on her thigh, squeezing and hurting her, I snapped. Charla's father, however, demanded I sit back down and not make a scene. I wanted to slap the shit out of him for allowing his daughter to be treated in such a way. He sees nothing wrong with it, and that pisses me off to no end.

What I did not know was, East was the largest donor of the night. He was the one who went up to the podium to give the main speech. He also told Corey in front of everyone in that room to take his hands off Charla. The entire place went silent.

East was smooth though, he dropped that shit and went right back into speech like nothing happened. All was quiet until he thanked Charla as his girlfriend. The gasps spread throughout the ballroom like wildfire. Charla's face turned beet red and she ended up storming out.

Like I said, a complete shit show. There was no way I could go see Scarlett. Just too much shit. I'll touch base with her later. Right now, I need to check on Charla. I sent her numerous texts and got not one single response. Shit must have hit the fan worse after she left.

I knock a few times and get no response. Yes, I have a key, but she left with East and if she brought him back here, and I don't want to walk in on that shit.

I knock roughly a few more times as my patience starts to wear before the door finally fucking opens. There Charla stands, looking rough. Suddenly I feel unsure as to why I came.

"Um, hey, I didn't want to just intrude... in case..."

She waves me off. "He's not here."

"Oh." I take a breath, relieved. "So how did the rest of the night go, you know after you stormed off?"

Charla says nothing as I follow her into the kitchen. She starts making coffee, completely avoiding my question.

"I take it from your silence that you've heard the news then?"

No time like the present to add to her ever-growing pile of drama.

"What news?" Charla snaps, causing me flinch in surprise. Hell, she has no idea. I pull the article up on my phone, the one that shows a very intimate photo of her and East.

"Charla, someone talked to the press. Someone shared photos."

"What?" she asks as she snatches the phone from me.

Her eyes go wide. I can't tell if she is reading the actual article or staring at the photo. Doesn't matter. The photo is all that matters. It is one of her and East outside of The Red Society. East's face all up in Charla's neck. She was clearly lost in pleasure. It's such a private photo. One that someone took. Someone was watching. I don't bring that part up though. Instead, I decide comfort is what Charla needs.

"Don't worry, Char, this will all blow over."

Of course, as the lie leaves my mouth, someone pounds on the front door. Charla walks over and answers it. Her father. Should have known.

He walks in like he owns the place, all arrogant. It annoys me.

"Spencer, I'm going to ask you to leave. I need to speak with my daughter."

I look over to Charla, not really wanting to leave her.

"I'll call you later." She just puts on a show, smiling brightly. It's fake as can be. If anyone can read my best friend, it is me.

I can't help but stare at her a few seconds longer. There is something there, just out of reach. I want to say something, yet I don't. I remind myself that this is her battle. Not mine. Nodding, I head out. There is someone else I need to see anyway.

It takes me about thirty minutes to pull into Scarlett's apartment complex. I'm relieved to see her car in its normal spot since I didn't bother to text her to check to see if she would even be here. I just drove straight here.

Scrolling through my phone, I pull up her name and hit call. She answers on the second ring.

"Hello?

"I'm outside."

She hangs up, not saying anything. Maybe she's mad that I stood her up last night. I didn't mean to, and I fully plan to explain that to her. Why I feel the need to do so, I'm not sure. We aren't some official couple or anything like that.

A few minutes later, Scarlett comes walking out. Holy hell. Her blonde hair is piled in a mess on top of her head. She is in a black baggy sweatshirt that falls off the side of her shoulder and a pair of denim shorts. Shorts that are too short in my opinion. They show off her perfectly toned thighs. Thighs that I wouldn't mind wrapped around my neck while I feast on her pussy. There's just something about her. Something I want.

All too soon those thoughts are replaced by a scorned looking woman walking up to my driver side window. Putting the window down, I flash a smile.

"Hey."

"What do you want, Worthington?"

"We're back to my last name now?"

She is pissed, I get it. She has a reason to be. I stood her up. Scarlett says nothing, just glares at me.

"Okay, look, I'm sorry. It wasn't my intention to blow you off last night. I wanted to see you. It's just the event turned into a shit show, and I had to stick around trying to calm the madness."

Scarlett's shoulders deflate. "Why do you want to see me anyway?"

That's a good question. I can't quite answer it. I open my car door and she steps back, allowing me to get out.

"I just want to see you, is that okay?"

"I don't know, we really shouldn't. We live two very different lives and I don't need random people showing up. I don't like being watched."

"You're a dancer, people watch you all the time."

"Not outside of the club they don't."

"I'm not a random person. I thought we got past this when I gave you my first name and my number. For the record, I never give chicks my number."

"Wow, that makes me feel so much better."

Her and her smart mouth. Grabbing her wrist, I pull her in close and lean down to her ear.

"You should feel special. I usually only fuck women and then never speak to them again." I blow my breath over her ear before biting just below her lobe. "You are different to me. I keep coming back and I haven't even fucked you, Scarlett."

I feel goosebumps form on her skin. I am getting to her. I fully plan to fuck her and very soon.

"Spencer," she whispers.

"Do you work tonight?"

"No, but—"

"Pack a bag. You will be staying with me tonight."

"What? No, I can't."

"You can. Now go." I slap her ass once before releasing her. "You won't need much. We'll order take out."

"Spencer, I, I've..." She trails off, biting her bottom lip. She looks sexy, all nervous.

"What?"

Scarlett swallows before lifting her head high. "I've never stayed at a man's house before."

"Like never?"

"Never."

Holy hell. How did this beautiful woman fall into my lap? I was borderline stalking her, that's how. This will make tonight even better.

"Good. Now get moving. Time is ticking."

She nods before walking back into her apartment. Part of me wonders if she is a virgin. There's no way though. She's a stripper. She let me finger her cunt and she sucked my dick like a pro. No way she can be a virgin.

Right?

Chapter Fourteen

SCARLETT

IT TAKES me no time to pack a bag. I mean what could I possibly need besides a toothbrush and some deodorant? It's not like I own anything sexy to wear to bed. A raggedy old shirt and panties. That's all I got. I imagine there will be sex involved. At least I hope there will be. It's been far too long since I've gotten any. Not to mention that the last guy I slept with was way below my standards. It was for a couple grand. If only I wasn't so desperate for money at the time, I would have never stooped so low. He was much older and completely grossed me out. Afterward, I went home and scrubbed myself nearly raw. I couldn't wait to wash him away. At the end of the day though, rent was paid. That's all that mattered.

I catch a glimpse of my mother when I step into the hallway. She's headed my way. Dread instantly fills me.

"There you are! I was calling your name. Why must you ignore me?"

She must be drunk already, she never called my name.

Not wanting a confrontation, I give her a puzzled look. "I'm sorry, I didn't hear you."

"You need to clean those ears of yours." She tsks. "I need some money. I am out of supplies."

By supplies she means alcohol. I bite my tongue to keep my anger clamped down. "I'm sorry. I paid the electric bill yesterday. I will not have any money until payday."

It's a lie. But she'll never be able to tell.

"Dammit, Scarlett. I really need supplies. Are you sure you don't have a twenty you can spare?"

"Not unless you don't want me to fill up my car tomorrow before work."

She waves a hand in the air. I can actually smell the stench coming from her. Vodka is her choice of poison today.

Lovely.

It makes me glad to be leaving.

"I'm sure your car will make it a bit without needing gas. Don't you think?" I watch as my mother plasters on a smile in hopes that I will cave.

"No, Mom, I must put gas in tomorrow or I won't make it to work. No work means no money."

I make to move past her, but she grabs my upper arm. "You know if you just worked a little harder, you know put in more hours, you might just have more money."

She lets go and shrugs her shoulders before heading to the bathroom. I stand there holding back everything I want to scream. I hold it all in. She won't listen. Never does. Shaking my head, I head for the door when I hear it. I stop dead in my tracks.

My mother is searching for stashed money. Opening

and closing the cabinets. She'll go to my room the minute I leave. I can't have her going in there. The last time she went on a search, she found a locked chest. It was nothing fancy, pretty small actually, but it had what small amount I had saved. Maybe eight hundred. She took a hammer to the box while I was at work one night. Blew every damn dollar. I came home to shards of wood all over the kitchen table.

I know what I need to do.

I quickly retreat back to my room and lock the door. I don't need her coming in while I'm stuffing cash in my bag.

I go to the first hiding spot. Inside my bottom drawer, I keep a small amount of cash stuffed in my socks. I pull out eighty bucks and stuff it quickly in my bag as a text comes through.

What is taking so long?

SHIT. Spencer is still outside waiting. I forgot about him waiting on me while dealing with my mom.

Sorry, I'll be out shortly

NEXT SPOT I rush to is my closet. It's small and I don't have a door on it. Mother dearest ripped it off while in a drunken craze. I reach for the only jacket I own. Florida doesn't get extremely cold, but on rare days, I at least have this one. There's an inner pocket. I reach in and take out the dollar bills. I don't bother counting it. Based on my mother's yelling, I probably have less than two minutes to find my last stash before she comes pounding on my door.

I go over to my window. The blinds are thin and cheap. But in the space between the wall and blinds, I'm able to hide a few bills when folded just right.

Sad, I know. This is how I live.

I grab the money, stuffing it in fast before zipping it up. Just as I get to my door, the pounding starts.

"Scarlett! I think you're lying."

I sigh, swallowing the anger that is now mixed with fear. I drop the bag behind my door as I open it a little.

"Mom, listen, I just picked up a shift tonight. I need to go so I can make money."

"Oh, good. That means you'll make tips in cash. I expect money to be on the table when you get home." She beams like she just won the lotto. It makes me sick. It makes me angry.

"Oh and Scarlett, make sure you put in the work so that you make a decent amount. The better you work it, the more you will make and we both know based on what you bring home now that there is room for improvement."

"Mother." I grind my teeth together. "I work harder than anyone in that club. We would have more money if you didn't need alcohol all the damn time."

I don't mean to lash out, shit maybe I do. I'm not sure. I'm fucking exhausted with this life.

"Scarlett! That's no way to speak to me. I have done so much for you. It's your turn to pull weight. Now get moving before you are late and that boss sends you pack-ing." I watch in disbelief as my mother turns on her heel and retreats to her bedroom.

Bitch.

There is no other way to describe her.

Sighing, I grab my bag and rush out the door. When I yank the door open, I nearly run into Spencer. His arm is raised as if he was getting ready to knock.

"What took so long? Are you okay?" Concern laces his words.

I shake my head pulling him away from the shit-hole life I live. Maybe a night away won't be so bad. I can pretend everything is okay for one night.

Chapter Fifteen

SCARLETT

WE DRIVE in silence for a few minutes before I hear Spencer sigh.

"Are you sure you don't have a boyfriend back in that apartment?"

A laugh escapes me. I can't help it. This rich dude thinks I got some boyfriend and that he is the reason for my problems. If only.

"No, I do not have a boyfriend. Believe me, I wish that was my only problem in life."

Shaking my head, I stare out as we leave my dump of a town behind. We are headed toward the ocean. I should have known. Of course, he lives out this way. Who wouldn't live on the beach when they ooze of nothing but wealth?

"Are you going to tell me what's going on with you?"

Spencer's question pulls me from my thoughts. I chew on my bottom lip while debating if I want to be open with him or not.

I decide the latter.

"No. Let us not make this personal. We don't really know each other." I'm still unsure of his motives, especially after that other guy showed up knowing my name.

"You don't want to get to know me?"

"I'm not sure yet." No reason to lie to the guy. This could be a night of sex and nothing more. A night that is long overdue for me.

We pull into some private parking garage. Another sure sign that Spencer Worthington has money. I shouldn't be surprised, yet I am.

He exits the car immediately after putting it into park, and comes around to my side where he opens the door for me. Like a true gentleman.

"Are you nervous?" he asks as he guides me to a set of elevators. The kind you have to swipe a key card for before they even open.

I don't respond, not until the elevator doors close and the numbers light up with each floor we pass.

"I am now," I state honestly.

Spencer steps in close, caging me in. The number five lights up as he leans in close.

"You have no reason to be nervous, Scarlett."

His minty breath hits my face as his words send chills down my spine. How can I not be nervous? I am spending the night with a rich man who for some unknown reason wants me.

Spencer breathes me in once more before the elevator dings. He steps back allowing me to go first. I glance at the number on the way out. Tenth floor. Seeing as there are no more numbers on the pad, I am assuming this is the top floor.

When we reach his door, my heart rate spikes. What will happen from here? I have so many questions, and not a single answer.

"Welcome to casa de Worthington."

"Is that what you tell all the women you bring back here?" I ask, laughing while shaking my head at the man in front of me. I stop short when I notice the serious look on his face.

"What?"

"I never bring women here who I just fuck once. No need to make shit personal with them if I do not plan to see them again."

Oh.

Well then, that was unexpected.

I swallow, unable to produce anything intelligent to say. I mean I want to ask if he plans to see me after this but based on his firm words, I am going with yes.

I guess I'm just not used to this type of thing.

"Let me show you around."

I smile and nod, following him through his elegant condo. He walks over to a large window and pulls back dark gray curtains. The sun has already gone down but the moon glows out over the ocean. What a sight.

"I chose this place for this view alone."

"Why the top floor?"

"To be away from people."

"Are you a loner?"

Spencer shakes his head. "No, I just like my personal space and not having people in my business all the time."

I guess being rich comes with a cost. I have no idea what having people in my business is like. I am no one.

"Come."

Spencer grabs my hand and pulls me down a wide hallway. Much wider than mine.

We reach the last door on the right. He turns the knob
and steps back.

I walk in slowly. There is a huge king bed. A thick gray
comforter covers it. I am beginning to think gray is his
color.

Across from the bed is a white dresser with an attached
mirror. A luxury I have never known. His room has double
glass pane doors that open to the ocean.

So many reminders of how different our lives truly are. I
turn to face the man in front of me. He is studying me,
rubbing his chin.

"What is so special about me?"

I've already asked this, I know. Yet, I still need clarifica-
tion because this just doesn't make sense to me.

"I already told you. There is something about you. Is it
so hard to understand that I want to spend time with you?"

"We are not the same. We live vastly different lives."

He steps into my personal space and reaches for my
chin. He lifts it to where our eyes meet.

"Stop comparing our differences. Let's just enjoy each
other, okay?"

"Okay." I decide to just roll with it. Even if it is for one
night.

Spencer leans in like he's about to kiss me and pauses.
"You enjoy being with me, right?"

"So far."

"Then it's settled."

His lips find mine. First, I taste mint, then him. His kiss

is firm, powerful. His tongue invades my mouth with no regard. I like the assault though. Our tongues continue to mingle, intertwining with such need. It is unfamiliar to me.

I don't recall ever being kissed like this. At some point I feel his hand leave my chin and wrap around the base of my neck, pulling me to where our bodies touch.

I can just make out the hard ridges of his chest but get distracted by his lips leaving mine. His departure leaves me breathless.

"We better eat before continuing this."

"What if I'm not hungry?"

Spencer smirks, his eyes full of lust. "You need to eat if you want to survive the night with me. You will need the calories." He winks once and pulls out his phone. "Take out sound good?"

"Uh, yeah, take out is good."

"Good. I'll be right back. Make yourself comfortable."

He walks out while typing away on his phone. I have no idea what he is ordering or if I will even like it, but I'm certain it will be forgotten the minute we continue where we left off.

Spencer comes back in like nothing just happened. His eyes no longer hold the hunger we were both feeling minutes ago. I won't lie, it leaves me feeling a little deflated, considering I am wound so tight and could use a release. I want nothing more than to get lost.

"How about we go back out to the living room, and you can tell me a little about yourself?"

I slowly nod. I really do not want to talk about myself. I do not want him to know what a pathetic, poor girl I am.

"Don't look so sad." He grabs my wrist pulling me in

close. "If we stay in here, I'll be tempted to do things and the food will go to waste."

"Fine, but I want to hear about you before I go divulging my secrets."

"Okay, but be prepared, I will *learn* all of your secrets."

I try to shake the thought of him knowing the real me. I like pretending better. It's what I'm used to. I pretend on stage every night.

All thoughts are forgotten as he kisses me on my neck as we walk back to the living room. It sends goosebumps down my spine. I fear it will be hard to keep my secrets locked tight with him doing things like this.

Chapter Sixteen

SPENCER

WHILE WAITING for dinner to arrive, I told Scarlett about me and life up to this point. Yeah, I was born with a silver spoon in my mouth. I won't sugar coat. My father's wealth paved the way for me. Eventually, I branched off, making my own way, and now here I am.

Now that dinner is here, it is her turn to open up. I want to know why she is so closed off. She has to be hiding something. Why do I care? I am not sure. I haven't figured that part out yet.

"So," I say as I swallow my first bite. "Did you grow up around here?"

I watch as she tenses for just a split second. She recovers quickly with a fake smile. Smart girl thinking I didn't catch on. Unfortunately for her, I did.

"You could say that, near where I live now. I was raised by my mom, a single mom. We moved around often but stayed in the area."

"That must have been hard."

Scarlett says nothing, just shrugs as she takes another

bite. I can't imagine moving around. I went to the same school from primary through high school. One giant private school. The best in the tri-county area they say.

I contemplate my next question while watching her eat. She studies her food and scrunches her face just before taking a bite. I suddenly fee like an ass. I never bothered to ask if she likes Chinese food.

"What's wrong? Do you not like it?"

"What? No." Her eyes go wide, giving her lie away.

"Scarlett, you don't have to eat it if you don't like it. I can order you something else."

"It is not that. Really. It's fine. I just..." She trails off, not finishing her sentence.

"What?"

I watch as she sighs before sitting back to look me in the eyes. "I have never had takeout before. It is different, but I do like it."

I am not sure I heard her correctly. She can't be serious.

"You've never had Chinese food? Like ever?"

"No, Spencer. Never. I told you we live very different lives. I grew up with a single mother, remember?" She waves a hand in front of her, annoyed.

"I'm, I'm sorry. I'm not judging. It is a little bit of a shock to hear."

And it is. If she has never had something as simple as takeout in a brown paper bag, that means she has not experienced much else. It makes me sad for her, but at the same time, it does not. Because that means I get to show her all these things. Does that make me a prick to think like that?

Yes. Yes it does, and I couldn't care less.

"You said no boyfriend?"

"No."

"Why not?" I'm curious. How can someone as gorgeous as she is not be tied down?

"I don't really have time for one and not many guys want to date a stripper." She replies so matter of factly.

I nod, chewing my food.

"Do you like stripping?" I raise an eyebrow.

She glares at me, not answering.

"What? It's a legit question."

"I love dancing. Always have. Do I love dancing while nearly naked on stage in front of a bunch of men? No."

"Then why do it?" I am sure there's plenty of other places she could work if she hates her job so much. Working for that ass of a boss probably doesn't make it easy either.

Scarlett slides her container back, placing her napkin on the table next to it. "I do it because it pays the bills. It pays the rent and puts some food on the table."

She excuses herself, taking her leftovers to the fridge before washing the fork she was using. She cleans up after herself. I like that about her.

While finishing my last bites of sesame chicken, I think about her words. That run-down place that she calls an apartment can't be that much each month. She lives in a crappy part of town. It cannot be unaffordable. She drives an old beat-up car. I doubt there is a payment on it. There has to be something else going on. Maybe she has a child to care for.

I get up and repeat her moves, putting my leftovers away and washing my fork. She leans against the counter, studying my every move.

"Do you live alone, Scarlett?" The words leave my mouth before I can think twice.

"No. I live with my mother. Are we done playing twenty questions?" She steps up close to me. Her snarky words catch me off guard as she steps up to me, grabbing my cock, not letting go.

Her bold actions turn me on. It makes me want to bend her over the counter and teach her who is boss. My cock twitches and I know she feels it because she winks once.

"For now," I grit.

"Good. I would like to freshen up and pick up where we left off."

I grab the back of her blonde hair fast, tilting her head back. My lips find her neck. Trailing light kisses down to the base of her throat. I feel her release me as she sucks in a breath. Just like that, I regain control.

Letting go of her hair, I step back and smirk. She is breathing heavy. I like what I do to her.

"Let's go shower, Scarlett," I say, unbuttoning my shirt.

She nods, not saying a single word. It makes me chuckle. That smart mouth of hers is fresh out of remarks.

Walking past her, I pull my shirt off, giving her a glimpse of what is to come. My damn dick is aching, begging to sink into her, and it will. Just not yet. I want to play with her before fucking her into oblivion.

I walk straight into my ensuite bathroom. All white. The walk-in shower has a small bench in the corner. I'm half tempted to bend her over it and give her a small taste of what's to come. Just the thought of her ass up while water cascades around it has my dick throbbing. It's damn painful.

Scarlett looks past me as she scans the shower. From the look on her face, I'm guessing she has never seen a shower as big as this.

"There's two shower heads?!" she asks as she continues to check out the space.

"There is." I have a rainfall shower head in the center of the shower, followed by a handheld massage shower head. "That one," I point to the handheld that's mounted, "will be used on your pussy in the best possible way. Now undress."

Scarlett quickly whips her head around, mouth wide open. I reach out with my hand, picking her jaw up off the floor, closing her mouth.

"I said undress."

I waste no time removing my pants and boxers. My dick stands at attention, hard. I watch as the beautiful blonde in front of me pauses, before reaching to remove her clothing. I do not help her. I could.

But I don't.

Once she's fully naked, I take in her perfect body. I know I have seen most of her body already. If I'm being real, it was mostly a blur. So much went through my mind during my private dance. However, now that she is in front of me and we are completely alone.

Fuck.

Her bare pussy is begging to be touched. Her tits are perky and perfect. Daring me to take a nipple into my mouth to suck.

Or maybe bite.

There is no maybe, there will be biting.

"Get in the shower, now," I demand before I lose all

willpower. Fucking her right here with her leaned up against my bathroom counter does not seem like such a bad idea, but it's not what I planned, and I always stick to the plan.

Scarlett lets out a nervous laugh. She's actually nervous. I can see it in the way she moves.

Good.

She should be.

Chapter Seventeen

SCARLETT

There's a tic in Spencer's jaw as he takes in my naked body. He could be annoyed. He did tell me to get in the shower and me being the person I am, I hesitate.

Is this a good idea?

"Scarlett," Spencer says through clenched teeth.

Fuck it.

I straighten, and walk into his shower. I nearly laugh. I have never been in a shower of this size, not one that's made of luxury. I study the shower head. The one that Spencer said he would be using on my pussy. Thinking about his words makes me clench my thighs together.

I feel him behind me as his erection slightly rubs against my ass. I push back into him on instinct. Why do I do it? I tell myself it is because I have gone so long without any sexual interaction. It's because I'm wound tight from all the stress that has been piled on me.

One night. I want one night to be carefree. To be wild. I owe it to myself. Hell, I deserve it.

"Easy, Scarlett."

"What if I don't want easy?"

Spencer's hands find the nape of my neck and pulls me back. His lips brush against my ear. "Are you testing me?"

I can't help but suck in a breath as he bites my ear once before letting me go. My clit throbs, begging to be touched at the words he has left hanging in the air.

I hear the cap pop open on whatever bottle he has in his hand. Seconds later, he is lathering my back, washing me. It's both shocking and soothing.

The scent of his body wash fills the now steamy air. Cool and refreshing, just like the ocean. That's what it reminds me of.

"Turn around," he demands.

I do as he says, looking him in the eyes. There's a fire there, burning bright. He stares back at me for a few seconds before moving his eyes to my neck. He brings the black cloth up and starts washing me. When he reaches my chest, he swallows slowly, clenching his jaw. I don't know how he does it, but he keeps his focus continuing on to my stomach. Meanwhile, I'm dying to be touched. My nipples are aching to be fondled. I want so badly to reach out and grasp his hard cock, yet refrain because I don't want to break his concentration.

The second he rubs the material over my bare pussy, my breath hitches. He smirks in response, rubbing it up and down a few times. Teasing me.

"Spencer." I go to reach for his cock, he moves fast, taking a step back.

"I'm not done bathing you."

There's a seriousness to his tone while his eyes are playful.

"The hell with washing me."

Spencer chuckles as he squats down to wash my thighs and legs. When he finishes with my feet, he drops the cloth and runs his hand up my leg. He circles the inside of my thigh repeatedly. The sensation is too much. I almost squeeze my legs shut.

Without warning, he slides a finger between my slit and starts rubbing exactly where I need him to. I moan out in pleasure, wanting, hoping for more.

All too soon though, he stands, cutting me off.

What the hell?

He reaches past me, grabbing the shower head. I had forgotten about that.

"Have you ever gotten off with one of these?" he asks.

My mouth drops open. He is so blunt.

"No. I've never been afforded such a fancy gadget." No point in lying. I've heard the girls in the dressing room gossip about using their shower heads from time to time. Never knew what the big deal was. It looks like I am about to find out.

"Good. That makes this all the better."

I watch as Spencer grabs his cock, stroking it a few times.

"I can do that, you know?" I nod to where his hand is wrapped around his erection. I wish he would let me touch him.

"You will. In time."

He releases his cock and turns the dial on the shower head. It is no longer a straight stream. Now it's streaming out close together, pulsating. I've never seen such a thing.

Spencer doesn't give me time to dwell on it though. He

holds it as the water hits my nipple. The water pelts me hard, massaging almost. And hell, if it doesn't feel good, sending electricity straight to my core.

He gives the other nipple attention, doing the same thing. It feels amazing. I fucking love it.

He moves his free hand between my legs, causing me to spread my legs further apart. The minute I do, the high power of water leaves my nipple. I nearly beg for more, until he aims it between my legs.

Fuck me.

I thought I loved how it felt on my nipples, but this. This is on another level. My clit throbs and the water pulsates over it. I reach up, rolling my nipples between my fingers.

"Feel good?" Spencer asks.

All I can do is moan in response as my eyes flutter close. I'm so close to coming undone. I've never gotten off like this before, but now I am seriously considering purchasing a handheld shower head. Even if I can't afford it.

He teases, bringing the shower head closer and then further back. With his way of teasing me, I will not last but another minute.

The water hits my clit exactly right and he holds it there, unmoving. I nearly scream out as my orgasm floods me.

And that's just what I do.

I scream out his name. God's name. I scream out so loud, praying to whoever will listen that I never come down from this high.

Unfortunately, the waves of pleasure slowly ease, and I reach out, palming the wall to hold my jello legs up.

Spencer runs a finger up my soaked slit. Soaked from the water, soaked from my orgasm.

He smiles and brings his finger to his mouth. Sucking on it. He stands and replaces the shower head, then turns it off. He walks to the other end of the shower grabbing two towels. When he turns to face me again, I can't help but stare at his erection.

"Dry up. I want you on my bed, on all fours."

He turns and steps out without saying another word.

Chapter Eighteen

SCARLETT

I DRY AS QUICKLY as my shaking hands will allow.

He wants me on all fours.

It takes me a few moments to gather the strength to think about moving. His words make me pause. I know I'm not innocent by any means. I've had sex plenty and in plenty of positions. I've done things for money that I'm not exactly proud of.

But this, this feels different.

Last thing I want to do is keep Spencer waiting though. Wrapping the towel around me, I slowly make my way out of his bathroom. I notice two things at once. Spencer is standing there, completely naked and completely hard still. The next thing I notice is the belt.

There's a black belt laid out on the bed. From here it looks to be a leather belt. Shit, who am I kidding. It's definitely leather. My eyes dart back to the man who just gave me the best orgasm of my life. Fire wages in his green eyes, a sinister smile plays on his lips.

One thing I am sure of is he plans to use that belt on

me. Whether to tie me up somehow or to punish me. The thought of both has me squeezing my thighs together.

Spencer notices. I know this because his eyes are now trained on my thighs. There is a tic in his jaw before he swallows slowly.

I take a few steps closer before pausing. Spencer's eyes pop back up to mine.

"I said I want you on all fours. Now," he demands.

"With the way you were looking at me, I thought maybe you had a change in plans." I decide to play it cool, winking as I walk past him. He slaps my ass hard, causing me to yelp. It damn stings.

"I don't change plans once I've made them. You'll learn that. Bed, now."

I nod and climb onto his gigantic bed. The mattress feels amazing under my hands and knees. I don't feel any springs whatsoever.

I feel a dip on the bed as Spencer comes up behind me. I can sense his eyes on my body, and it makes me feel exposed, being in this position.

"Still glistening," he says just as his fingers push through my slit.

My body instantly reacts to his touch. My back arches, letting him know I want more, even though I just got off. Spencer uses his finger to tease me while his other hand rests flat just above my ass. The second he removes his finger I feel empty, but only for a split second because, in the next, his tongue is on me. He swipes up my slit and back, repeating the process. I try to resist, but my body reacts on its own and my ass arches up to give him better access. I nearly grind my pussy into his face.

His firm hand slaps my ass hard before returning to hold me in place. It stings, but in the best way. Is that even possible?

I realize this man has me right where he wants me. That should scare me. Giving him all this control. Being reckless with a stranger.

Yet, it doesn't.

There's something about Spencer that makes me feel free. He's giving me the release I so desperately need. With each swipe of his tongue, my orgasm builds.

"Spencer," I moan as I start to feel myself teetering close to the edge. He stops suddenly and pulls back.

"You taste fucking perfect."

"Spencer, please."

He slaps my ass once more. "You coming from my tongue will happen, but not tonight."

My head hangs as he denies me.

His finger plays at my slit again when he begins to speak. "Don't worry, you'll get to finish and when you do, it'll be with my cock inside you."

His words light me afire. I'm wound up and will gladly take his dick. I vaguely hear the foil packet tear. Shit. I didn't even think about protection, I have been too hung up on desire.

The belt that is next to me suddenly disappears. Fear and excitement flow through my veins. I have no idea what Spencer's plans are. How does he plan to use it?

He gives me no time to think though. I feel his cock line up at my entrance. He doesn't push into me though. It's agonizing. I push my ass up, wanting him. The man behind me grabs my ass hard, stopping me. His tight grip will surely leave bruises.

"When I'm ready to dive into your pussy, I will."

I think I might combust. This is pure torture. Why can't he just get on with it and fuck me already?

Spencer runs the belt across my ass cheeks. I clench in response because well, frankly it makes me nervous, excited. Hell, I'm not even sure.

"Relax, Scarlett." He says it so confidently. Like his dick isn't lined up at my entrance. Like he doesn't have a leather belt in his hand.

I try to do as he says, however, it is easier said than done.

I hear it before I feel it. The belt cracks against my ass fast. Hard. A scream rips from my throat. The stinging is intense, until he drives his hard cock into my pussy. Slides right in because I'm so damn wet. A hand comes down over my ass in the exact spot that the belt hit seconds before and begins massaging slowly. It hurts but feels fucking amazing at the same time. Pleasure laced with pain. He moves slowly behind me, teasing me with his cock. Each time he pulls back a little more, to the point he's almost pulled completely out and then he thrusts back in.

It is absolute torture and I fucking love it.

Little moans escape my mouth as he keeps this rhythm up. I try to move against him, to get him to move faster because my pussy is screaming for more. I need more.

"You'll come when I want you to come," is all I hear before another whack from the belt hits my ass. This time the opposite cheek. I can't help but scream out in shock or pain. Maybe it's both. I am not sure because as he starts massaging, he thrusts harder, faster. I'm soaked. I can hear the embarrassing sounds but am quickly overtaken by the tightening that's forming low in my belly. I'm not going to last.

"Spencer!"

The belt hits my ass one more time and that's all it takes for me to come undone. Screaming out his name, my pussy clenches around his cock as I drown in ecstasy.

I vaguely hear the growl that leaves Spencer's mouth as he thrusts in harder than he ever has before stilling. He's breathing is heavy and hot across my back as he leans over me.

I realize that I have been missing out because I've never been fucked like this before.

Chapter Nineteen

SPENCER

After slowly pulling out of Scarlett's cunt, I excuse myself, heading into the bathroom to clean up. I come back out with a wet cloth for Scarlett and the sight of her causes me to stop in my tracks.

"What are you doing?" I ask through gritted teeth. Scarlett is wrapped back in the towel that she had earlier and she appears to be kneeling, digging through her bag. Totally normal except for the fact that there's money spilled out of the bag.

Not my money. I'm certain of that.

Scarlett stills at my words. Standing straight up. The look on her face is one of shame and embarrassment.

"Words. I need words," I state as I walk closer. I'm still naked and I don't even care.

"I... I was looking for my clothes." She looks back to the cash and that's when I see it. Shame. Definitely shame.

"Why do you have all that money on you?" I'm genuinely curious.

She says nothing, just shrugs her shoulders before kneeling again to stuff it all back in there. That's not good enough for me. I'm a man who needs answers, facts. I need, no scratch that, I want words.

"Scarlett, why do you have all that money on you?"

"I just do." It's barely a whisper. If I wasn't paying such close attention I would have missed it. I walk up, grabbing her upper arm, I gently pull her up to face me. I don't want to scare her. Especially after taking my belt to her perfect ass.

The towel around her body falls to her feet. As much as I want to let my eyes roam her body for the hundredth time, I need her to see me.

"Scarlett, I just claimed your body and you want to shut down on me now?"

A sigh leaves her lips before she straightens. She holds her head up high before she speaks. "I have to carry it on me to prevent my mother from stealing it."

Well shit, I wasn't expecting that. I don't know what to say to that. I mean I think it's pitiful that this woman has to carry her pay with her because her own blood would steal it.

Scarlett turns, kneeling. I give her space to allow her to finish putting the money back in her bag. An idea comes to mind. It's probably fucking stupid considering we don't really know each other, yet I'm going to offer it anyway. I stare at her as she stands up, this time with her clothes in hand.

"If you need a place to keep your money safe, I have an old safe I'm not using."

"Ha, no thanks." Scarlett laughs as she passes me to head into the bathroom. I forgot I had a cloth for her, so I follow her and put my hand out before she shuts the door.

"What are you doing?" she nearly snaps at me. I'll allow it for now, but that shit isn't going to fly with me.

"I had brought this for you, you know to clean up," I say, holding out the cloth.

"Oh, thanks."

"Scarlett?"

"What?"

"I'm serious. You can program the code for the safe. I won't have access to it."

"Yeah, no thanks. I'm not just going to leave my money at some rich guy's house."

"Wealthy," I correct. "Regardless of what I am, the offer stands."

I remove my hand and turn to walk away to find sweats. She may not trust me yet, but she will. It's just a matter of time.

Taking the belt to her was step one. She trusts me somewhat to allow me to do such a thing. Random women do not let some guy they barely do such things.

I'm determined to claim Scarlett. It'll only be a matter of time.

I'm lying on my side of the bed when Scarlett comes out in faded black yoga pants and a crop top that barely covers the bottom of her tits. I sure as hell hope she doesn't go out in public like that. Anger starts to bubble up at the thought. She puts herself on display enough stripping, I hope like hell she covers up more when she's not at that club.

She pauses in the doorway, unsure of what happens

now. All women do it. I've seen that awkward after-sex expression more times than I care to count. The only difference is that those expressions happened in a random hotel room and not at my place.

Might as well clear the confusion up right now though.

"Come to bed, Scarlett."

She doesn't say a word, she just climbs in on the other side, pulling the gray sheet up to her waist.

"Now what?" She's blunt. I like it better when she is sassy, and confident.

"Now we sleep." I pause for two seconds. "For now."

Her mouth gapes open. I caught her off guard. Good.

Winking once, I reach over and shut off the light. I roll toward the gorgeous woman next to me and pull her into me. She's breathing fast and I know it's because of me.

I don't let my hands roam her body. As much as they are itching to fondle her nipples, to dip my hand below the waistband of her pants, I refrain. My dick is semi-hard already. Having her ass up against it sure doesn't help. It's taking everything to not lose all control and rip her clothes off just so I can taste her sweet cunt again. To swirl my tongue around her pebbled nipples before biting them.

Fuck.

Now my hard-on is raging, and I know she can feel it. She doesn't say a single word, doesn't make a move. Actually, her breathing is starting to even out a little. That's what I want. What I need. I need her to sleep so she'll wake up later with me between her legs. I want her to wake up screaming my name while I feast on her.

That's my plan.

Fighting the urge, I try to think of anything but fucking

her. It's hard. There is something about this woman. Something familiar, yet not familiar at all. I don't know what it is but her perfect body up against mine has me rethinking my plan. I never rethink. I know. I always know.

So why do I feel like I'm on the edge of losing control just so I can fucking taste her all over again?

Chapter Twenty

SPENCER

I slept long enough to recharge. I wake up with a raging hard-on. Probably the same one I went to sleep with.

I listen for Scarlett's breathing, she's still asleep. Sliding away from her, I pull the sheets back a little. With the moonlight beaming in through the sheer curtains, I am unable to see much. I even left the blackout ones open on purpose. I want to be able to see what I can.

Very slowly, I pull her yoga pants down her legs. She stirs, but only briefly. Her bare pussy is only inches from my face as I carefully grip her hips to give me a better position. If I tilt my head slightly, the glow from the moon hits her just right.

So perfect.

Without wasting another second, I lean down and run my tongue along her slit. Her leg falls open more. I swipe again and again. She stirs a little more with each swipe of my tongue. Her scent, her taste. It should be forbidden. I keep swiping, swirling, and every so often I pause to suck on her now swollen clit. Little whimpers leave her mouth begging me for more. Little does she know, her desperate pleas are like music to my ears. My cock strains, begging to stink into her pussy.

Sliding one finger into her wet cunt, she arches for me. Such a good girl with the way her body reacts to me. It's like her body was made for me to worship. Made for me to fuck.

And mark my words, I will be fucking her again. Very soon.

My tongue works over her most sensitive parts as I feel her legs start to shake. She's close and once she comes all over my mouth, I'm dragging her sweet ass to the edge of the bed where I plan to fuck her until the sun comes up.

It does not take long before her hands find my hair. Her whimpers are now moans that have me feeling like I could blow my load right in my sweats. I wouldn't care either.

"Spencer!" she screams as her back arches.

The minute my name leaves her pretty lips, I know she's close. I thrust my finger into her, moving fast, while I suck on her swollen bud. She clenches around me while pulling my hair. Scarlett screaming my name over and over as I lap up every delicious drop only adds fuel to the raging inferno inside of me.

I don't let up though. No, I suck her clit as her screams fill my bedroom. Hell, I wouldn't be shocked if the residence below me could hear her.

Only when her hands leave my hair and fall at her sides, do I finally let up. I peer up at her sleepy eyes. Desire stares back at me. And as I planned, I grab her hips, pulling her to the edge of the bed.

I sit up fast enough to lose my sweats. Wanting to waste

no more time, I line my dick up at her entrance. Her pussy glistens for me. It's a damn sight. I slide right in.

"So tight for me," I tell her as I sink balls deep into her.

Scarlett says nothing, only throwing her head back in what appears to be total ecstasy.

I pound relentlessly into her, knowing she'll be sore by the time I'm done. All part of the plan. I want her to feel me which each step she takes. Even while she's at The Red Society baring it all.

She reaches up, clawing at my chest. A tinge of pain sends electricity straight to my balls causing them to tighten. It feels good. Her marking me. It's almost too much. But I'm not ready yet. I glance toward the window. The sun isn't quite up enough. Almost.

It's almost time.

And that's what I focus on for the next few minutes while pounding into her. I focus on her moans and how she begs for me to go harder and in the next to stop she can't take it.

I don't stop.

Call me fucked up. I don't care because I know in her next breath she will ask me to fuck her harder all over again.

When those exact words leave her mouth, I fuck her harder than I've probably fucked any woman before her. Most women are vanilla, but I knew after our little bit of fun in my car that she wasn't like most. That she would take everything I dish out.

Maybe that's why my obsession is growing.

I need her to come apart again for me. Reaching down, I pinch her nipple. Hard.

Scarlett screams out, digging into my chest harder.

"That's it. Fucking come again for me. This time on my dick."

"Oh my god. Yes!"

I move to her other nipple and repeat the process, pinching her hard. Just like that, her pussy clamps down as her orgasm hits.

"Spencer, fuck! I can't take anymore."

"Ask me to finish then," I demand as I once again feel my balls tightening. This time I know I won't be able to hold off and that's okay because the sun is starting to rise.

"Spencer, please. Fucking come. I can't!"

Her screams fall into whimpers as I thrust in hard as I fill her sweet pussy with my cum. I don't stop, thrusting hard until I've emptied every last drop into her.

"Fuck," she says as she lays there sprawled out on my bed as I pull out of her. Cum drips out of her pussy. My cum. I'm not sure exactly why, but the sight of it has me wanting to fuck her all over again.

Scarlett will be mine, I tell myself again.

Can one become addicted this soon? This quick? I don't know why I'm becoming obsessed with her. There's just something about her. I can't put my finger on it. However, when I do, there will be no going back.

"Shit, Spencer." She breathes heavily. "You didn't use a condom."

No, no I did not. I wait for regret to wash over me. She's a stripper, I should have at least asked if she's clean. I assume she's on the pill. It wasn't even a thought as I watched my dick enter her and now that I've had her bare, I'll never use one.

Regret doesn't come.

Scarlett rolls over and eyes me. Her eyes are full of questions. Questions I need to answer.

"I did not. I'm clean though."

She sighs. "I'm clean, and on birth control too, but still." The blonde laid out before me sighs, throwing her arm across her face, shielding herself from me.

"Don't do that. You can't hide from me." I reach out, removing her arm from her face, surprisingly she doesn't put up a fight.

"I'm not hiding, Spencer." She laughs nervously. "What are we even doing? We don't know each other from shit and here you are not using protection when we have sex. It's insanity."

She has a point. I can't explain, this pull I have toward her.

"Scarlett, I had your pussy in my face. I feasted on you like it was my last meal. I already told you that I wanted to get to know you. Stop overthinking what this is or isn't and let's just enjoy each other." I lean down a bite her nipple gently, before finding her beautiful eyes staring at me.

"Okay," is all she says.

I hear her stomach growl and know right away she's starved.

"Let's go shower and grab some breakfast."

"That sounds like a great plan." She giggles.

I stand, holding my hand out, and she takes it, pulling herself up. I watch her as she walks to the bathroom before me. She has that just fucked walk. A sense of pride fills me. I did that.

I glance back at the bed, cum is smeared on the sheets

from where it was dripping out of her. Those will need to be washed.

Guess I'll put a call into the housekeeper.

Chapter Twenty-One
SCARLETT

I HAVEN'T SEEN Spencer since he dropped me back off at my apartment. That was nearly a week ago. We have chatted a little via text which has been a welcome distraction considering no one texts me, but the reality of what we did keeps haunting me. It shouldn't, yet it does.

The Uber driver pulls into The Red Society and instead of having the driver pull around back where the employees park, I have him drop me off at the front. I don't need some stranger knowing where I live and that I actually work here. I nearly laugh at the thought. Spencer found me easily enough. My face is bare and I'm in a plain tee and jeans. Hopefully it's enough of a casual look that I don't "look" like a stripper.

When I walked out this afternoon to head in, my back tire had a flat. Something I really didn't have time for. Or money for, and I know I will need to deal with it, but for now, I am here, not late.

Paying the driver, I step out without so much as a word. The driver doesn't waste any time pulling out either, he's got places to be and money to make I assume. I start heading toward the huge doors when I hear my first name come from behind me.

I freeze.

"I was hoping to see you again."

I turn suddenly. It takes me a few seconds before it registers. He's the guy from my apartment. A nervous shiver runs through me as I stay silent.

"Don't look so surprised. I don't bite. I mean I could bite if you want me to." The man's dark eyes roam my body once. It makes me feel nauseous, especially when he licks his lips.

"What do you want?" I ask, trying to sound confident. I fail.

"I have an offer for you. A job. Good pay."

"What is your name?" I ask, already knowing he probably won't give it to me. There's something about this guy. He's hot. Charming even with his blonde hair styled perfectly. I bet women flock to him, but something rubs me wrong. Standing there wearing a pair a navy slacks with a navy and white checkered button-up, he looks sharp.

He pauses and continues to study me. I don't like it. Not one bit. It makes me feel grimy, just like the first time I met him. He makes me feel dirty, almost like he knows he is better than me. Of course he is, but that is only because he is rich.

"Never mind, don't bother with your name." Ah, there she is. I knew I had a backbone. "I'm not interested." He walks up fast before I can finish my sentence. He stops. He is too close to me. I go to take a step back, but his words make me stop.

"I know you can use the money, Scarlett." He says my name slowly, very slowly. How the fuck does he know that about me?

Suddenly, the front doors burst open and I turn to see my boss marching over. Relief and fear wash over me.

"Well look who it is?" I hear the condescending tone in the man's voice as he speaks to Mr. Sinclair.

"You are not welcome here, you need to leave." My boss looks at me, he's not very happy. "Lettie, inside."

I nod and rush toward the door. Glad to be getting away from this bizarre situation.

"It was nice talking with you, *Scarlett*."

I dead stop in my tracks. I turn, not bothering to look at the man. No, my eyes go straight to my boss. He's staring at me. Fury is written across his face. I know without a doubt that I will be reprimanded.

"Inside, now," Mr. Sinclair demands, pointing at the doors. This time I rush inside and don't look back.

I've just barely made it to the dressing room when his voice comes over the intercom. "Scarlett, my office. Now." He doesn't hide his anger.

The room falls silent, and I plaster on a fake smile, shrugging my shoulder at the girls as I walk past.

"Sir, you wanted to see me?" My voice is shaking as I stand in his doorway. I know I'm in trouble. We have rules here. Rules I technically didn't break, but they were still broken

All because my tire was fucking flat.

"Sit." That is all my boss says.

I do so quickly but can't help the nervous feeling

growing in the pit of my stomach. Please don't let me be fired.

"Why were you outside with Corey Richards?"

So that's his name? I open my mouth to tell my boss that I didn't even know him but stop myself because I have a feeling that would look a thousand time worse.

"Now, Scarlett. I don't have time for this," he snaps.

"He, um... offered me a position." I internally groan. That doesn't sound much better.

"He offered you a job?"

"Yes, sir."

"Why on earth would you give him your real name? You don't know him from shit."

I shake my head. "I... I didn't. He already knew it. He called me by it as I was walking in."

My boss starts pacing behind his desk causing me to worry about just who Corey Richards is. He's lost in thought for a minute. Hell, it feels like forever before he stops and makes eye contact with me.

"Why did you take that photo of Charla and me outside and submit it to the tabloids?"

Photo? What is he talking about? "I'm sorry, what photo?"

"Don't play with me. Why did you submit it to the damn tabloids?" Anger ripples from him as he slams his hands on the desk, causing me to jump.

Confusion runs through me. I'm so damn confused. About everything that has happened up to this point.

"I don't know what you are talking about. I don't know anything about a photo."

My boss studies me. Like really studies me. He doesn't

take his eyes off me. He tilts his head as if he is trying to figure me out. There's nothing to figure out.

"Sir, what are you talking about?" I ask to break the awkwardness that is clearly growing by the second.

"Give me your phone."

"It's in the dressing room."

I dropped my bag on my vanity the second I made it to the dressing room. I watch as Mr. Sinclair pages for Marc. He asks him to retrieve my phone and bring it up to his office. What could he possibly want with my cell phone?

"Scarlett, is there anything you are keeping from me?"

"Sir. I swear I don't know anything about a photo."

How we moved on from Corey, whatever his last name is, to a photo is beyond me. The night hasn't even started, and yet I'm ready for it to end. I'm not sure I can take much more of the shit show that has become my life.

The voice in the back of my head says it became a shit show the minute you met Spencer. I shake the thought not wanting to believe that.

"Sir, I am seeing someone. I did meet him here initially, but he has been a complete gentleman." A gentleman who is rough in bed. I don't say that part out loud of course.

"Who is it?"

I swallow. "Worthington, Spencer Worthington."

"Fucking hell," he says as he swipes a hand through his perfectly dark hair. He says nothing else. Just stares at me. Not like Corey though. This is different, though still weird.

The awkward moment disappears as soon as Marc walks in and hands me my phone. I unlock it right away and hand it over to my boss. I have nothing to hide. He's quiet as he goes through it.

"You have no photos at all?"

I shrug. "What would I take photos of?" Kind of sad to admit. It's the truth though. It's not like I live some glamorous life that I want to post about all over Instagram. Nope. Not a chance in hell you find a selfie of me in my ratty bathroom.

My boss studies me silently as dread fills me again. He's debating.

"Am I being fired?" I can't help but ask, my voice on the verge of cracking. I'm typically a strong woman, however, I need this job. I can't lose it.

"If I catch you associating with that piece of shit again you will be. Don't you ever bring him here again." His words shock me.

That's not what happened.

"I didn't bring him here. He was already here when I arrived."

"Is that so?"

Holding back tears, I nod. Please God, don't let me get fired over a stranger. I had no part in him being here. Please. I expect it over Spencer, but not some fucker I do not even know.

"Tell me something about yourself, Scarlett."

"I'm sorry?" His change in demeanor confuses me yet again.

"Tell me something personal? Something only you know."

"Um, there's not much to tell. I mean I did just tell you I am sort of seeing someone and you already know my mom worked here years ago."

"She did. She ever mention your dad or past relationships?

Why is he asking about my mom and her shit relationships? Does Corey have something to do with her? Fuck, I feel like I have whiplash from all the subject changes tonight.

Shrugging, I tell him, "Sometimes when she is drinking, she'll mention stuff. Most of it makes no sense."

"Like?"

"I don't know. Once she mentioned my birth dad being wealthy. Another time she mentioned he was famous, or like a judge, something like that, and that he had my sibling." I roll my eyes. "I usually don't pay attention when she rambles. It's probably all lies anyway."

Waving my hand, I laugh and shake my head. Who pays attention to a drunk woman rambling about a lifestyle she never lived?

Chapter Twenty-Two

SCARLETT

Staring at my reflection in the brightly lit mirror, I apply my bubblegum pink lipstick. It's almost showtime. As confident as I am in what I do, I am dreading it tonight. Between what happened outside of the club with that man and then the game of a hundred questions with my boss, I'm mentally drained and my thoughts are all over.

Maybe it's because you had a perfect gentleman worship your body. I know that none of the eyes out in the crowd will look at me the same way Spencer did as he claimed all of me. Not a single one.

Marc comes across the speaker. "Lettie, you're on in eight."

Leaving all thoughts of Spencer behind, I lift my head high as I stand in my clear sky-high heels. A skimpy rhinestone bra and thong are the only things that cover me.

I hear Tia whistle from across the dressing room and laugh.

It's showtime.

I COUNT my tips while waiting for the Uber driver to text me to let me know that they have arrived. This time I made sure to tell them to pull up out back. I don't need another damn scene.

It's a good thing I earned a decent amount tonight. Paying for a driver twice in one day nearly guts me. I need every single dollar that I dance for. Paying for a driver is not in my budget. Not now and probably not ever, yet here I am.

The second my phone dings, I stand putting my money away. It's not the Uber driver, but Spencer texting me.

> When can I see you again?

I CAN'T HELP the smile that forms on my face. How do I reply to that? What I want to say is "how about tonight?" The problem is, I don't want Spencer to think I'm desperate.

I don't know what this hot man sees in me. Not a damn clue, and when he sends me such a text it gives me hope. Hope for what, I'm not quite sure.

Before I can decide how to respond, a second ding comes from my phone, this time it's the driver.

I tip the nice female driver, refusing to meet her eyes as I get out of the car. I already know what I'll find. Pity. Picking a stripper up from her job and dropping her off at this shit complex is bad enough. I don't even bother to look back after exiting her compact car.

Sighing I head for my place, pulling out my keys. I had sent Spencer a text on the way here with a simple word.

Soon.

While unlocking the door, I try not to let it bother me that he hasn't replied. He could be busy I tell myself. As soon as I walk in I regret it. The fucking disaster in front of me has me wishing to be back at Spencer's and in his arms.

My mother is passed out on the couch and it fucking reeks. Beer bottles are everywhere. Beer means she couldn't afford the heavy stuff.

I grab a few empty bottles as I walk past and head into the kitchen. This place is gross. Tossing the bottles into the overflowing trash, I can't help but wish for more out of this life. I want to blame the wealthy man that brought me into his house, showing me the type of luxury most only dream about.

That would be a lie though. I can't blame him. There's only one person to blame and she is currently out cold on a ratty ass couch.

Am I wrong for blaming my mother? The woman who gave me life and raised me alone?

MY MOTHER SCREAMING and banging about in the kitchen wakes me instantly. Not that I slept well. I tossed and turned, checking my phone every few minutes hoping to find a text. One that never came.

"Scarlett!"

Sighing, I drag my ass out of bed as my name is called several more times.

"Yes, Mother?" I say as I open the bedroom door.

"Where have you been? I ran out of money, and you were nowhere to be found!"

I must remind myself to count to three and not roll my eyes.

"I have been working. One of us has to work. The bills won't pay themselves."

I'm not in the mood. I brush past her to head into the bathroom, but she catches my arm. My eyes instantly go to hers. She is glaring at me, with a snarl. I'd love to wipe it off of her face. Just once. For everything she has done to us. Everything she has put me through, continues to put me through.

I don't.

"I don't know what has gotten into you. You have been an ungrateful bitch lately and I won't stand for it. Do you understand me?" My mother applies a little more pressure on my arm and smiles. I know she thinks she is hurting me. What she doesn't know is that her grip is weak. I've had dirty old men that were drunk as fuck squeeze my arms and thighs harder. I won't even say how tight Spencer has grabbed me.

Yanking my arm from her grasp, I smile sweetly. "You could try being grateful too."

With that I walk into the bathroom, quickly locking the door behind me. I start the shower, stripping right away. I only have minutes of a decent shower. No time to waste.

My mother continues her yelling from the other side of the door, but I hear none of it. No. Instead, I choose to block out her ranting and visualize my time with Spencer. I imagine I'm back in his shower with his hands on me.

Fuck, I hope he responds to my text so I can escape this hell hole.

My mother is gone by the time I came out of the shower, along with the twenty I left on the counter last night. I left it after cleaning up her mess in hopes that she would leave me alone this morning. Ha. She always has to have the last word. Whatever, I don't have the time or energy for her. Rent is due and I need to go drop it off before figuring out my damn tire.

The second I turn to head for the office after locking up the apartment, my name is called. I freeze, my blood running cold. I know the voice. It is the man from last night. The voice that could get me fired.

Fuck.

"Scarlett, over here."

I follow his grimy voice to a slick black car. He's leaned up against it. I don't make a move for him right away.

I glance around at my surroundings, before looking him over. He's hot. I'll give him that. Blonde hair that I'm sure has been grabbed a time or two. He is dressed in a dark suit that has not one wrinkle. He stands tall, legs crossed at his ankles.

"I don't have all day, Scarlett. We have business to discuss."

I shake my head as I walk up to him. I hold my head high as I reach him. "Why are you here?"

"I told you, I came to offer you something. Money that you can't refuse."

"Doing what?" Placing my hand on my hip, I give him a

little attitude. I don't want him to think I'm hard for money even though something tells me he already knows I'm dirt poor.

"Tell the press you are dating East Sinclair."

I scoff. "Excuse me? You can't be serious. I don't even know your name. Why would I do that?" I turn on my heel. I don't have time for this crazy shit.

"Ten thousand."

I stop, frozen in place.

"Ten thousand dollars to go to the press. Tell them you are dating your boss. That's all. No details need to be shared."

Ten fucking grand.

That's a lot of money to me. Well to me anyway.

"Name's Corey."

It could be my fresh start. A way to get out of this damn hole.

Ten thousand dollars to lie to the newspapers? I can do that. What's the worst that can happen?

Chapter Twenty-Three

SPENCER

SOON.

That one word had driven me nuts all week. Not to mention the countless times I ended up jerking off in my shower because every time I stepped into it, all I could picture was her naked body and the way she came apart for me. So easily too.

Soon.

Fuck that word. I'm going to her apartment tonight. I am sick of waiting. I will have her.

Flicking the light switch on my way out of the office, I catch Charla's light is still on. I groan running my hand down my face. She needs to go the fuck home and deal with her mess.

"Charla," I say, while trying hard to hide my annoyance.

"Yeah, Spence?"

I take a deep breath. I hate how she gives me that sweet voice. She is lucky she is my best friend.

"Promise me you will close up and go home within the next thirty minutes?"

"Uh, yeah, sure."

Her lips tell a lie.

"Fucking hell," I mumble under my breath as I nod and leave. There is no point in trying to talk any sense into her. Charla is trying to find her way. She's finally standing up for herself and I'm not about to argue with her.

Once I'm in the car, I shoot Scarlett a text. I hope she isn't working at The Red Society tonight. I'll wait if I have to. I really hope that won't be the case. I don't bother waiting for a reply either as I head out toward her place.

A huge sigh of release leaves my mouth the minute I spot her car in the parking lot of her apartment. Picking up my phone, I see that she texted me back. A few times actually.

Tonight?

I'm not sure tonight is a good night.

Spencer? Did you mean tonight?

SOMETHING IS UP.

TWO WORDS. That's the only reply I give her.

Now I wait and it better not be long. She has me on edge now.

Not only do I wait. I fucking wait over ten minutes.

With my hand firmly on the door handle, I'm on the verge of getting out of my car and knocking on her damn door. I'm not usually an angry person. Cocky, sure. Not angry though.

However, for some reason, when Scarlett defies me, she makes me angry enough that I want to take her sexy little ass and bend it right over my knee. Punishing her is what I want to do.

Badly.

And that's just what I intend to do when I get her back to my condo.

Picking up my phone, I decide to bypass the texting bullshit and just call her. She better answer.

The line connects. She doesn't say hello. In the background, I hear a woman yelling. I try to listen in but can only make out muffled words. Worry begins to creep into my blood. It's foreign. I don't worry about other people, especially when I have never had to worry a day in my life.

At least not until her.

"Scarlett?" I say into the phone.

I get no response, but finally hear her voice.

"Mother, I am going out. I work hard all week. I can go out for a night."

More mumbling before Scarlett speaks again.

"I am an adult. You cannot keep me here. Stop."

I'm out of my car before I even process, all the while keeping my phone glued to my ear. Who the hell thinks they are going to keep Scarlett locked up?

My fist pounding on the door sounds through the phone. The voices fall silent.

"Scarlett!" I yell, not even caring that I sound like a lunatic.

Shit. Maybe I am turning into one.

And it's all because of her.

Silence comes from the other side of the door. The two women fighting have gone quiet. So I try again. "Scarlett, open the door."

I know I sound insane making such a demand. I don't give a fuck. She needs to open the door and she needs to open it now.

It seems like eternity before the lock turns. The door cracks open and a face peers out. It's not Scarlett.

An older version of Scarlett stares back at me. Her hair is mostly gray. The blonde that is left, looks dirty and unkept. Her eyes are wild. A clear indication that she is on something. They do not sparkle like Scarlett's.

"I'm here for Scarlett," I state so matter of factly.

"Who the hell are you?"

The stench of stale beer that leaves her mouth nearly makes me gag. I close my mouth fast and I grind my teeth to keep from lashing out at this woman. She's drunk.

From this moment forward, I feel it is my duty to never let Scarlett become this woman.

Never.

"I'm a friend." That is all I give her.

"Yeah, well Scarlett doesn't have visitors."

Hearing her say that secretly brings me joy. I'll never admit out loud that I like that I am the only one.

"She does now. Go get her, I don't have time to waste."

The drunk woman stares at me, well she tries her best to give me a nasty look but fails. I smile in return.

She backs away from the door, swaying as she goes. She does not close it, but also doesn't invite me in either. I wait, unsure of how to proceed.

"Scarlett," I hear the woman holler from a distance and know then it's safe to enter.

Pushing the door open with my foot, I take in the sight in front of me.

"Holy fuck," I whisper.

The stench hits my nostrils first. I can only compare it to a mixture of garbage and vomit. That is not all though, the view inside Scarlett's apartment is sad. Gross even. The air is stale. There's nothing in my direct line of sight that makes this shit box a home. No family photos on the wall. Nothing personal at all. In fact, the walls actually look grimy.

Scarlett comes into view and stops dead in her tracks the second her eyes land on me. Fear and embarrassment flash in her eyes before panic sets in.

"Spencer! Who let you in? Never mind, wait outside, in your car. I'll be right out." She rambles so quickly that I nearly miss the tears forming.

"Scarlett," I say as calmly as I can. One of us needs to remain calm. "Get your things. You are not staying here. Not with her."

I keep my eyes on the gorgeous woman who stands in front of me. She is beautifully broken.

Scarlett nods as the first tear falls. She turns and rushes back down the hall. I'm half tempted to follow her just so I can keep an eye on her. Instead, I stand in the doorway unmoving.

When she comes back not even a minute later, I walk up and take the bag from her.

"Did you grab your money? You will not be leaving it here."

"Spencer."

"No, don't Spencer me. Go get it now. All of it."

There's no way I'm letting her leave any amount of cash behind. Not with a crazed woman. She is drunk and who knows what else. It's clear she's addicted to something and Scarlett has suffered enough.

As far I am concerned this shit needs to end and it needs to end now.

Chapter Twenty-Four

SPENCER

No words are spoken during the entire drive back to my place. We do not need words. What Scarlett needs is time to gather her thoughts. I decide to leave her alone with them. Who am I to give my two cents? I won't lie, I want to. And maybe I will, but not right now.

Pulling into the parking garage, Scarlett sighs. It's sad.

"You can stay with me as long as you want," I say, without giving it a second thought.

"Spencer, that's very nice, really. But I can't leave my mom."

"Yes, you can. You are an adult."

"I told you, you don't understand. It's complicated."

Without elaborating, she gets out of the car, closing the door. I groan in frustration. Why can't she understand that she doesn't have to stay and put up with that shit? It's infuriating. I take a deep breath before getting out of the vehicle to go around and meet Scarlett.

All this frustration, there is only one way to make it all

disappear and that's being buried in her pussy with her screaming my name.

I am finally calm when we reach my floor. I still feel the tension between us, but I have calmed down enough not to slam her up against the door and fuck her right then and there.

"Shower. I'll order dinner."

Scarlett pauses, not saying a word. She only nods and heads for my room. Good girl.

Scarlett is still in the shower and the food has arrived. I'm guessing she needs time to wash the shit with her mom away. However, I'm growing impatient.

Setting the food on the kitchen counter, I head in her direction. The mirror is fogged over. I can see her silhouette through the glass. Her head is tilted down standing directly under the spray. My dick hardens. It shouldn't, yet it does.

I quietly pull my shirt over my head. Scarlett pays me no attention as I finish undressing. I don't join her in the shower; instead, I reach in and grab her blonde hair. Not quite rough, not exactly gentle either.

That sweet sound that leaves her lips has my dick jumping. I can't wait to sink into her.

I say nothing as I pull her wet ass out of the shower. I turn her around, pushing her against the counter. Her reflection meets mine in the mirror. The puzzled look on her face turns me on further.

"Spencer," she goes to question me, but I silence her words when I rub my dick against her ass.

Reaching between us, my fingers find her pussy and hell if she isn't soaked.

I waste no time spreading her legs. I line my dick up and drive straight into her.

Fuck.

She feels fucking amazing.

I reach around, grabbing her throat. She swallows hard. Her eyes find mine and what I see has me fucking her harder with each thrust.

I half expected to see fear staring back at me. Surprisingly, it is not fear that I find.

What I see staring back at me through the mirror is lust.

Pure fucking lust and I love it.

I squeeze a little tighter and I'll be dammed if her pussy doesn't tighten around me. The sensation is too much but I keep thrusting into her while gripping her throat.

Scarlett's whimpers can hardly be heard. I know she's on the verge of an orgasm, so I squeeze a little bit harder.

"Give it to me," I demand.

And she does.

Her eyes roll as her pussy clamps hard around my dick. The satisfaction of making her come apart with my hand around her throat sends me over the edge.

My hand drops from her throat, falling to her hips. I dig my fingers in roughly as I come hard. Her wet hair falls around her face, blocking my view.

When I pull out of her, she sighs. When moments go by and still no words are said, I begin to worry that maybe I have gone too far. Crossed a line. I hope not.

"Scarlett," I say, unsure of how to proceed.

Finally she lifts her head, pushing her hair away from her beautiful face. I watch completely confused as a smile grows across her face in the mirror.

"Thanks, I needed that."

What? Did I hear her correctly?

She turns my way, pats my chest and steps back into the shower as if I didn't just fuck her with my hand wrapped around her neck.

If she hadn't captivated me before, this seals the deal. I cannot let her go.

I will not let her go.

Not a chance in hell now. She lets me unleash the beast and doesn't question it. Doesn't judge me.

The only delay now is convincing Scarlett that she is good for me and that we can work.

That's a battle for another day.

Chapter Twenty-Five

SCARLETT

I PAUSE before unlocking the door to my apartment. I dread what is waiting on the other side.

My mother.

After a night of the best sex I have ever had, I made Spencer drop me back off to deal with the one person I can't seem to let go of.

I owe it to her, I think.

Between her and the lunch that I am supposed to attend here shortly before work, I'm a mess. Am I doing the right thing? What even is the right thing anymore? The lines of working to survive have blurred to the point that I'm not sure about anything anymore.

I take a giant breath and open the door.

First the smell hits me. It's disgusting and vile as if the trash hasn't been taken out in days. It hasn't. I know this because I'm the only one who cleans up anything around here.

The second thing that hits me is how quiet it is.

"Mother?" I call out as I stuff my keys in my back pocket. When I get no response, I start to get anxious.

She's probably just passed out like usual, I tell myself.

When I reach her room, I'm surprised to not find her but feel relieved too. She's not lying in bed dead. That's good at least.

I grab my bag for work and drop a twenty on the table. That will hold her over.

It will have to.

I'm applying my mascara when my name comes across the speaker. The voice on the other side is angry and that can mean only one thing.

He knows. He knows I told the press that it was me in the photo.

I keep my head down as I walk to his office. I don't want to see the pathetic look on anyone's face. The shame I have been feeling for days is enough.

Once I reach his door, I hesitate mid knock. "Sir?"

"Come in." The tone of my boss's voice makes me want to tuck my tail and run. I don't though. I need this job, and even if it is too late, I will beg to keep.

I walk in on shaky legs. I feel like an idiot for what I have done. Ten grand sounded so good. If only I had really thought the repercussions through.

Mr. Sinclair stands. "Why, Scarlett? After all I have ever done for you. Why are you trying to destroy me? Did that bastard put you up to it?"

"Sir, I'm sorry. I know you have done so much for me.

Still do. Am I..." A hiccup escapes as I start to cry. I can't help it. With all the shit that has come up recently, I break down. "Am I being fired?"

"You didn't answer my questions. Why did you do it?"

"I didn't want to. I didn't really. Honest. That man offered me a lot of money to say it was me in the photo. I figured it would be no big deal."

"How much did he offer you?"

"Ten thousand. Mr. Sinclair, you know I need that money. You know how beneficial it would be." I sound so desperate. It's ridiculous.

My boss stares at me for a minute before speaking. "Did he come through with the money?"

As if this can't get worse. I hang my head. That fucker didn't come through with any cash and I'm in the hot seat. I'm the one on the verge of losing my job.

"He never paid you? For lying?" he asks before slamming his hands on his very expensive desk.

"He, he promised he would send payment as soon as the article was printed. I am... um... waiting."

"Fucking hell!" my boss shouts. "Go home, Scarlett."

Oh my god. No.

"What? am... I... No, please no. Don't fire me."

"I didn't say I was firing you. I told you to go home. Go home before I fire you. You deserve to be fired. Fucking fired to never return." His words are mean. Cold. The look on his face is anything but nice. He looks hurt and angry. Both at the same time. Of course the anger trumps the hurt. It should not shock me, given our history. Yet, it does. Even though everything we have done in the past was strictly platonic, it still hurts.

I can't help that I'm full-on crying. I can't afford to lose this job at all. I need it like I need my next breath. I'm so damn stupid.

"Leave now!" Mr. Sinclair shouts angrily.

"I'm so sorry, sir." And I am. I'll do anything to prove it too.

"If he contacts you, and I mean contacts you at all, you call me right away. Understood?"

"Yes, sir," I say quietly before turning and walking out of his office.

The entire drive home I cry. I cry over the disappointment my boss has in me. That man has done more for me than the father I have never known ever has. Hell, he has done more than my own mother has ever done for me. That's just sad.

My phone dings. I glance at it and see Spencer's name. I can't deal with him right now. My life is a shit show and involving him is the last thing I need. Sex is great and all, but reality is we will never be anything serious. Can't be.

So, I do what I do best. I ignore him and all thoughts of him.

Chapter Twenty-Six
SPENCER

SCARLETT IS AVOIDING ME. I'm not exactly sure why that is. I swore I saw Corey Richards pulling out of her apartment complex a few weeks ago and then shit hit with the newspapers. I don't know why, but something tells me he is involved. Charla's father too.

I am concerned for her well-being. I'm also concerned for my best friend too. Her father is a snake. Cold as fucking ice. He'll stop at nothing to get his way.

Needing a break from work, I open my social media and the first thing I see is a gossip headline. I read it once. Twice. FUCK.

Without thinking, I leave my office and rush straight to Charla's. I don't even pay attention to the chatter around me.

I barge straight in without knocking. Not that I need to, I own this place after all.

"Charla! You need to see this shit!" I spit out so fast.

Charla doesn't even glance up from her computer. "Not now, Spence, I'm in the middle of this account." She waves me off like whatever I have to say is no big. For once she has a fucking backbone, however, now is not the damn time to blow me off.

I slam my hand down on her desk. Hard. "Fuck that account, Charla. Shit is going to go down. You need to read this!"

She finally looks at me. "Jesus, Spence, what is it?"

Shoving my phone in her face, I nod for her to read the headline.

Mother of East Sinclair, Owner of The Red Society, being released early next week after serving almost twenty years for child abuse.

I watch the color slowly drain from Charla's face and come around to stand behind her. I watch as her body trembles and put a hand on her shoulder hoping to calm her all while knowing it won't.

I may not like East and he has caused quite the uproar but he's been good, caring to Charla. This news is going to light a fire and I'm not sure it will be able to be controlled before burning everything in its path.

"Charla, this is going to blow up. I think you need to stay at my place until this blows over. You don't know how Sinclair is going to react."

"What? No. If anything, he's going to need someone."

Immediately she grabs her cell. Her slender fingers move fast across the glass. I watch for a minute to see if East's horrible past sinks in. It doesn't because she stands gathering her shit. She doesn't understand the severity of this.

I need to stop Charla before she makes a beeline for the door.

"Char, wait... I'm serious. You don't know what can of worms and past trauma has just been opened up. You could be walking into a ticking time bomb, and I don't think it's safe." I grab her upper arm in hopes that she is hearing what I am saying. Fucking please hear me.

"I'm not scared of East. He won't hurt me."

"I don't trust him." And it's true. I don't.

Charla smiles at me. "I know you don't. But I do."

Her smile. There's something about it. Almost familiar but different. I shake my head and let go of her arm. I watch as she rushes out of her office, headed for the one place East Sinclair can be found.

The Red Society.

I PULL into the Red Society, it's just after six o'clock and the lot is still dead. I don't spot Charla's SUV. Good.

I drive around back and don't see Scarlett's either. Also good. I don't want her here. I can't tell her that though. She's so much more than taking her clothes off for a dollar. She just fails to see that. Hopefully soon I will be able to change that.

Pulling out, I drive in the direction of her apartment. There's a pretty high chance that she'll be there.

Sure enough, her car is parked directly in front of her door. I'm not going to bother with a text. I get out and go straight to door, knocking twice. At least this time I don't hear yelling. It's quiet.

A minute late the door cracks open. Beautiful green eyes stare back at me. Confusion written in them.

"Scarlett."

She glances behind her before stepping out and shutting the door behind her. "Spencer, hi, what are you doing here?"

"You've been avoiding me," I state as I pull her into me. Fuck, how I have missed feeling her against me.

She sighs. "I'm not avoiding you, I've just been busy." The lie rolls off her tongue. Way to easily and it pisses me off.

"Pack a bag, tonight you're mine."

Scarlett backs away and looks like she wants to fight me on it, but I'm not having it. I point to her front door. "Now."

She laughs, shaking her head before turning to go inside. I stay where I'm at. Waiting.

I hate fucking waiting.

For her though, I wait.

When she comes out with her ratty bag, I reach for it right away. "Let's go." Then I grab her wrist, pulling her along.

"Okay, okay, Spencer. I'm coming." She nearly laughs again before speaking. "I can use a distraction for the night anyway."

As I toss her bag in the backseat and then hold the passenger door open. Scarlett goes to get in but I grab her hip, stopping her. Her back is to me as I lean in close to her ear.

"Baby, let's get one thing clear. I'm not just a distraction. Understand?"

I hear her breath catch before she swallows. She nods. That won't do. I want fucking words.

I release her hip and grab her pussy. The seams of her cheap black leggings threaten to split. I don't care either.

"I'm not a distraction, Scarlett. Is that clear?"

"Um, sure?" she questions.

I am almost certain she said that with a smirk across her face. I squeeze harder and a moan leaves her lips.

"Scarlett, don't toy with me."

"Why not? I love it when you punish me," she states as she leans her ass back into my now hard dick.

Fucking hell.

This woman.

Chapter Twenty-Seven

SCARLETT

I can still feel the heat of his hand. It makes me squeeze my thighs tighter. The drive to his place takes forever. At least it seems that way. It could be because I'm now hot and horny.

Damn him.

Spencer turns down the music. "Tell me, why have you been avoiding me?"

He's not going to give it up. I look out the window debating how much to tell him. Will he judge me? Probably not. Spencer has been fucking me and bringing me back to his place for a while now. Why can't I just trust him and be honest?

"I'm waiting. No lies. Now tell me," he demands.

"Life is complicated right now." It's not a lie. Life is so fucking complicated, and that asshole still hasn't paid me what he said he would.

"Scarlett, stop beating around the bush."

"Fine, I screwed up. I lied to the local newspaper about

being the chick in the photo with my boss. It's caused some problems at work."

There I said it. Out loud for the first time. God, I'm such an idiot. I drop my face into my hands to hide my embarrassment.

He gasps. "Why on earth would you do that? That ass of a boss could fire you."

My head snaps up in annoyance. "You think I don't know that? I didn't do it for the hell of it, believe me. I would never do that to my boss. He's all I have."

"You have me." Spencer nearly grinds his teeth.

I sigh, unsure of what to say to that. I've never had someone, a guy no less tell me that I have them. That I can rely on them.

"Why did you do it?" he asks, clearly needing an answer.

"I was offered a lot of money to go to the papers. I could use the money, thought it would be no big deal."

"How much?" His voice is void of any emotion as we pull into his parking garage.

"Ten grand."

Spencer hits the breaks so hard my hand flies out slapping the dashboard. "Shit!" It nearly gives me a mini heart attack.

The man next to me turns and stares at me. The expression on his face makes me nervous.

"Ten thousand dollars? You were offered ten thousand to lie to the newspaper?"

I nod, not wanting to make eye contact. When he says it like that, it makes me feel gross, stupid even.

Spencer grips my chin forcing me to look at him. There's fury in his eyes.

"Who the fuck paid you to do it?"

"A... a man," I stutter.

"What fucking man, Scarlett?" Spencer is angry, I can feel it in his grip. I can hear it in his tone. I can see it in his eyes.

I must be broken because I find his anger thrilling. It thrills me to the point I have to shift in my seat while attempting to squeeze my legs even tighter.

"Answer me!"

"Um... a man similar to you, rich, fancy car. He told me his name was Corey." I roll my eyes. "If that was even his real name."

Spencer's hand drops from my chin. Both hands find the steering wheel gripping it hard as he hits the gas hard. It takes him no time to pull into his designated parking spot. The silence makes me anxious. I'm not exactly sure what to think.

It feels like an eternity before he finally releases his steering wheel. He kills the engine and gets out without so much as a word.

I was hoping the subject was dead in the water since he hasn't said anything else. However, that sliver of hope is crushed the second Spencer corners me in the elevator up to his penthouse, condo, or whatever it is called.

"I don't want you speaking to him EVER. AGAIN. UNDERSTAND?"

"I don't plan on it, as soon as I get my money—"

Spencer cuts me off. "You haven't been paid?!" The rage radiates off of him like the sun radiating off of a mirror.

I swallow, not liking where this is going. "Not yet, I haven't seen him."

Saying that out loud really hits me. The reality is, I don't even know how to reach this Corey dude. I may never see him again. I am so damn stupid.

"Fucking hell, Scarlett." He steps back from me and runs his hands through his hair. Perfect timing too because the doors to the elevator open.

He walks in a rush, dragging me by my wrist. I nearly have to run to keep up. I would ask what the rush is, however, I'm pretty sure he wants to get me behind closed doors so he can do whatever he wants with me.

And that's perfectly fine with me. Like I said, I could use the distraction.

The second the door is closed behind me he shoves me against it. His mouth bites at my neck, my ear. It sends shivers straight to my core.

"I don't want you talking to that fucker. Stay away from him," Spencer says while continuing to bite at me.

"I have to get my money first."

"No, you will stay away from him."

I freeze, he doesn't understand. He was born rich. He could never understand. "Spencer, I will stay away, just as soon as I get my money."

Suddenly, I'm being lifted as if I weigh nothing and thrown over his shoulder. He turns, walking fast.

In the next second, I'm being tossed on top of his fancy couch. He wastes no time as he rips my leggings down my legs. His hands find my black thong next, tearing them like they were made of nothing. I watch as Spencer loosens his belt and undoes his button. The man in front of me shoves his pants down exposing his hard cock. Precum beads at the tip. I bite my lip in anticipation of what is to come.

Spencer pulls me to the edge, lines his cock up, and drives into me so hard. I cry out. Pleasure laced with pain is what I have grown to love. I grab a hold of his dark hair as I throw my head back.

He's rough and doesn't let up and he fucks me harder than he ever has. I didn't think that was possible, but here we are.

"See what happens when you don't listen to me?" His words hold bite, yet I'm not scared. In fact, they do the opposite. They turn me on further.

"You will be punished, Scarlett."

Electricity spreads throughout my body, hitting me just where I need it most. I need him to keep talking, to keep making demands.

I lean back and smirk. "Maybe I like being punished."

He doesn't respond and for some reason that drives me mad, so I tug his soft hair harder. "Did you hear me? Maybe I like being punished."

He pulls my hair, forcing my head to snap up. "I heard you. Loud and clear. You don't know what you are asking for."

His hard thrusts don't let up. It's pure agony, I'm so close and he's not giving me the release I'm so damn desperate for. I tug his hair harder.

"Scarlett," Spencer says through clenched teeth.

His hand leaves my hair and begins circling my clit. The moan that escapes my mouth is anything but quiet. Hell, I don't really care how loud I am at this point.

I feel the rush of my orgasm approaching at the same as Spencer pulls out of me. He grabs me by the hair and yanks me off the couch, forcing me on my knees in front of him. I can barely register what's happening when he grips my jaw, opening my mouth. He shoves his cock in my mouth and starts thrusting so hard, my eyes water instantly as I try not to gag. My hands dart out, to grab the back of his thighs so I have some sort of leverage.

Spencer fists my hair while continuing to pump in and out of my mouth. He's anything but gentle. My pussy throbs between my thighs. How he fucking left me on edge should have me boiling, but I asked for it. I asked this gorgeous man to punish me and here he is delivering.

"Are you ready to listen?" Spencer growls as his cock hits the back of my throat.

I attempt to shake my head, but his firm grip prevents me from doing so. I take every inch of him as he fucks my face. Tears continue to fall all the while I'm still dying for a release.

He doesn't give me any warning as he explodes inside my mouth. The salty taste hits the back of my throat as I swallow. I peer up through the tears and lock eyes with his. I expect to see lust, anger even. Instead, I am met with something I can't quite decipher. Before I can try to figure it out, he blinks, and erasing whatever it was. He pulls my hair forcing me to stand.

"Are you going to listen now?"

I shrug. "Are you going to get me off now?"

His finger finds my lip and he rubs a little bit cum that has pooled there. "So damn defiant."

I smile, but stay quiet because I swear if I don't get to fall apart to his touch, I might lose my mind.

"Get back on the couch, lay back."

I jump at Spencer's command and do as he says without hesitation.

His hand roams under my top until he finds my breasts. I'm not wearing a bra. A finger flicks my nipple once before squeezing it tightly. His fingers trace their way to my other breast. Just when I think he will repeat what he did to my left breast, he squeezes my nipple first, rubs it between two fingers. A breath leaves my lips in anticipation of his next move. The pulsating between my legs is back with a vengeance. More than ever do I want him to get me off.

Like right now.

Instead, though, his fingers dance across my skin ever so slowly and seductively as they make their way lower.

Finally, he touches my most sensitive spot, causing me to nearly arch off the couch.

His fingers nearly ghost across my skin. Ever so lightly teasing me. Barely touching me. Barely giving me what I need to get off. Honestly, it's more of a punishment than him shoving his cock in my mouth.

When Spencer finally begins to rub gentle circles on my clit, my eyes drift closed as my toes curl. I can practically taste my orgasm. It's right there out of reach.

His finger leaves my bud and is quickly replaced with his tongue. That first flick almost sends me flying. Spencer's hand slaps my belly, holding me firmly in place.

His tongue circles, teasing me. I can't fucking take it.

"Spencer, please," I beg, not caring how pathetic I sound.

I feel him smile against my skin as he sucks, and I lose it. I see stars. So many bright stars. My fists find his hair again as my body convulses. Incoherent screams leave my mouth.

After coming back down from the most beautiful high, Spencer pulls me up. He looks me dead in the face, an unreadable expression across his face.

"You are mine now."

My mouth drops open as he turns and walks off. I want to say something except no words leave my mouth. I have a feeling nothing I say would matter anyway.

My brain is in an after orgasm fog. Spencer is unlike any man I have ever met.

I'm just not sure if that is a good thing or a bad thing.

Chapter Twenty-Eight

SPENCER

THE REST of the evening with Scarlett was what I would call simple. We ate, fucked, and fucked some more. I dropped her off at her apartment this morning. I was sure to let her know that I no longer wanted her stripping. She laughed and said "You are crazy, but I'll think about it" before slamming the door, not even bothering to look back.

Hope swelled in my chest at that last bit. It is a far out request and not very realistic for her. I get that she has a fucked up situation and needs to make the money. Doesn't mean I have to like it. Hell, just the thought of her tits in some dude's face has me seeing red.

Pushing back from my desk, I decide I need a coffee.

Walking back to my office with two coffees, I have had time to clear my head and think. The fact that Corey has contacted and set up Scarlett says enough. Nothing good is coming.

I walk to Charla's office. She's not here yet, so I wait.

I see her approaching, her steps pause a second when

she notices me. When she reaches me, she gives a small smile. I straighten the second she says good morning.

"Charla," I say as I hand her one of the cups. Something about her hits me. I've known her for years. I know everything there is to know about her. My eyes don't leave her while I try to figure out what it is about her.

Charla clears her throat while looking at me, confused.

Shit, I'm probably scaring her.

"I'm worried about you. I have a terrible suspicion that your father and Corey are up to something."

"What do you mean?" she asks innocently.

If only she knew what I knew about Corey right now. How much do I tell her? Do I tell my best friend I'm fucking a stripper? No, not now.

"Look at the news. The pap is eating up your boy's past, dragging his name and his club through the mud. You think that was random? You think it was a coincidence that his mom was released early?"

"What are you saying?"

"Come on." Charla can't be that stupid. She is though. She was raised to stay in the dark, to follow without asking questions. "I just have a bad feeling that this might have been set up. Something isn't sitting right with me."

Charla sighs. "I don't know. Maybe, maybe not. I just wish it would all go away. The photo of me and him, his past stories. I'm so sick of being in the limelight."

"I agree. Sadly, though, unless you give into your father, it's not going to go away. You need to figure out how to handle it. Perhaps staying with me will help some."

I only say she should stay with me because I don't trust the men in her life. At least if she stays with me for a while,

I'll know she is safe. That and maybe one of the women in my life will listen.

"I'll think about it, Spence."

Her words.

Her words are familiar, like what Scarlett said this morning. They even sounded the same.

I stare at my best friend and try to piece together why they would sound the same.

Their eyes...

"Why do you keep staring at me like that?" Charla asks, ripping me from this startling realization.

"Sorry."

Shit.

"Fucking shit," I mumble to myself while shaking my head as I quickly leave her office.

It's nearly quitting time when a news alert pops on my phone. I changed my notification settings after the photo of Charla and East surfaced. I knew Corey and Stefan would be up to more shit and as I open the article, I stand correct.

Stefan is behind the early release of East's mother. There is a photo attached to the article. I zoom in.

Fuck.

A photo of East's mother with a woman. Her back is to the camera. Blonde hair flows down her back. I know right away who it is. It hits me. They used Scarlett to look like Charla. Frame Charla.

It is the perfect disaster.

This is bad. I may not like East but this is wrong. If he sees this, and chances are he will, it will set him off if it hasn't already. He will blame Charla, I know it. I feel it.

I march straight to her office. I must catch her before she leaves.

"Charla, you need to get your things from Sinclair. Come straight to my place after."

"What? Why?"

Why can't she just do as she's told? It pisses me off that she is even questioning me.

"Just listen to me for once and do what I tell you," I spit out. My eyes beg her to just fucking listen. I do not have it in me to tell her what a piece of shit her father truly is. I do not want to be that person. Not today.

Please, Charla, just fucking listen.

"Uh, okay."

"I'll walk you to your car."

Relief fills me as we start walking. That's short-lived though.

The minute she pulls away dread fills me. I should have gone with her. I could have at least gone with her to make sure nothing happens if East snaps.

Instead, I am standing here in the parking garage like an idiot.

Chapter Twenty-Nine

SCARLETT

I HAVEN'T SEEN Spencer for a few days. He sent me a vague text about needing to handle some personal affairs. Maybe he had second thoughts about telling me to quit my job. As if I would really follow such a command. In both our dreams maybe. I will not lie, his absence bothers me.

Whatever.

I shouldn't really be getting tangled up with him anyway. I need to focus on more important things. Like working, paying my bills, and keeping a low profile.

Surviving, Scarlett. Focus on surviving.

Pulling into The Red Society, I think about Spencer's words and look down at the envelope in my hand. I prepared a handwritten letter explaining why I want to give bartending a try. A page long, listing the reasons. I could try my hand at bartending. What is the worst that Mr. Sinclair can say? No?

As I head to the admissions office, I climb one stair at a time. Yes, The Red Society has an admissions office. Mr. Sinclair takes his club very seriously. No drug addicts working for their next high. Nope. This is not the place for that.

Each step closer to the admissions office has me growing more and more nervous. Stripping has always been my way of life. It is all I have ever done. I don't know how to do anything else. Just the thought has me both scared to death and excited.

My palms are sweaty causing me to drop my envelope right in front of Mr. Sinclair's doorway. I quickly bend down to grab it.

"Scarlett, could you come in here?"

Shit. I wasn't fast enough.

"Marc, you can go," he says as he waves off one of our bodyguards.

Marc gives me a nod as we pass by each other. He quietly shuts the door leaving me alone with my boss.

"How are you?"

"I'm... I'm good."

"That's good. Have you been staying away from Corey?" he asks and it seems genuine.

This is an easy question. I can do easy. "Yes, sir."

"Did he ever send payment?"

My heart sinks and I look down at my feet. I can't meet his eyes. No, that asshole never did and now I must admit that to my boss.

"No, he did not."

"I see," is his only reply.

Somehow, I find the courage to lift my head, brushing my blonde hair out of my face as I do. I find Mr. Sinclair studying me. It makes me more nervous than dropping off the letter in my hand.

He looks away and grabs his phone. He scrolls on it for a few. I watch for any emotion to show. He gives away nothing though and that is almost worst.

Suddenly, he places the phone on his desk and slides it toward me.

"Do you know this woman?"

It's a photo of me with my new neighbor. Corey arranged that lunch and my outfit. He told me he would pay me a bonus for attending and making her feel welcomed. Why does Mr. Sinclair have a photo of us? I wasn't technically around Corey again.

"Why do you have a photo of the two of us? That is my neighbor. You're not having me watched, are you? I told you I would stay away from that man." My words come out harsh. I don't mean for them to, I can't help it. Something isn't right.

"Of course not. Where did this woman say she moved from?"

I have to think for a minute. I don't think she ever told me. Our conversation was very minimal with simple questions about our lives.

"Um, I'm not sure she ever told me. Why? Is everything okay?" I try hard to swallow the growing panic, it is hard. Calm is the last thing I feel.

Mr. Sinclair clears his throat. "That woman is my mother. She was just released from prison. That photo was published in the local paper."

My hand flies to my mouth as my eyes find his. Just released from prison? What the fuck did Corey set me up with?

"What do you mean she was just released from prison?"

He smiles a sinister smile. One that sends chills straight down my spine and not in a good way.

"I was hoping you would ask. She abused me for many years. My grandfather rescued me from her hands. Surely you must remember this or perhaps your mother might have mentioned it. Have you not seen the news? The girls must be gossiping in the dressing room." Pain flashes across his eyes, but only for a second. He recovers fast and back in place is that smile.

They have been. I have heard bits and pieces, but truth be told, I'm too distracted. I haven't paid any attention between trying to keep my job and pay the bills, and Spencer. I don't engage.

I feel horrible now for having lunch with the woman.

"No." I answer as honestly as I can. "I'm sorry, I don't pay attention to those types of things. I have one focus and that's not losing my apartment."

Mr. Sinclair looks at me with pity in his eyes. "It seems we have something in common, we were dealt a shit hand as far as having a mother is concerned."

I nod. If that isn't the truth, I do not know what is.

He waves his hand. "You may go, but I'm going to suggest you stay far away from that woman. Especially if you want to continue here. Is that clear? There will be no second chances when it comes to associating with her." I hear what he is saying. Loud and clear. His mother hurt him in a way that there is no coming back from. Some wounds never heal.

"Yes, sir," I answer, standing fast. I want no part of being around her. She is very similar to my own mother and one is enough for me.

I make a bolt for the door, itching to get out of this office, but pause once I reach the door handle.

"Sir, I just want you to know that we only went to lunch that one time. I thought it would be nice to make a new friend. I haven't seen her since. Not once."

He gives me a sad smile. "Keep it that way, Scarlett. Oh and one more thing, I would like to gather a DNA sample from you."

I stand. "Yeah, sure of course." It is the least I can do considering all the bullshit I have recently caused him.

I leave and head back down the stairs. All thoughts of dropping off the envelope in my hand have been forgotten. I will never get the position now.

Chapter Thirty

SPENCER

Charla is staying with me. I haven't seen Scarlett. Things have been intense. What I was not expecting was to notice certain things and the longer my best friend stays here, the more I see it.

A resemblance.

It's ludicrous, these thoughts. Charla and Scarlett just have the same hair color. I lie to myself.

As I stand out on my balcony, I peer out at the ocean. I spot her right away, sitting on the beach. Can't miss her. Her blonde hair drapes down her back. Just like Scarlett's.

Fuck.

My doorbell rings. I can only guess that a certain someone is here for her since I am not expecting anyone.

I shake my head the second I open the door and see East standing in front of me.

"She's not here," I say flatly.

"I'll wait."

His words annoy me for some reason. "Why?"

"Because we have a lot to discuss."

"Fine, I'll go get her. Just wait here." I shut the door behind me. He can wait in the hallway. I am not letting that fucker snoop my place while I am not there.

I'm unsure if I should let her know East is here. She has not been herself and to be honest, I'm concerned she will either cave and run back to him or she will go back to following her father's orders. Neither would be good in my opinion.

By the time I reach her, she is no longer sitting with her ass in the sand. No, now she's standing waist deep in the water. I stand back and just watch her.

For the first time ever, she looks carefree. It's as if she's freed herself from all life's troubles. If only that were true though.

She rides a wave in, and I can't help but laugh at how ridiculous she looks. She stands looking toward our condo and pauses the second she notices me.

The closer I walk, the more the resemblance between the two women in my life grows. I have had Scarlett wet and naked in my arms. Charla stands in front of me, her hair wet. She's wet...

"Hey—"

"This is new. Since when do you swim in the ocean?" I ask, needing to silence the thoughts in my head. Seeing Charla like this, I don't know, it stirs something. Something I have never felt before with her.

"I don't know, something came over me and I decided to go out. Want to join me?"

She shrugs her shoulders and my eyes fly to her chest.

Fucking hell.

"Definitely not. Besides, you need to come back up to

the condo, someone is waiting for you, and um, yeah, your shirt..."

Charla looks down, noticing what I've clearly seen. Her tee hugs her chest tightly and hides nothing. Nothing at all. Her pink lace bra leaves little to the imagination.

Ugh. I feel myself growing hard. I need to look away before this gets worse.

"Did you say someone was waiting for me?" she asks like her fucking see-through tee is no big deal.

I can only nod.

"Who? Because if it's my father I'm not up for seeing him."

"It's not your father, now come on. You can have my shirt." I quickly lift my shirt over my head and hold it out for her. She doesn't take it right away, leaving me no choice but to make eye contact. She smirks before looking me up and down.

Well this is new. My best friend is checking me out. I should not have these weird feelings coursing through my veins right now. She doesn't even try to hide the fact that she is checking me out.

Charla steps out of the water. She pulls her tee in an attempt to ring out the water, but it only makes it worse.

"Jesus, Char, next time wear a swimsuit or something." I nearly grind my teeth as I turn away.

Charla grabs the shirt from my hand and I finally feel free enough to walk away.

Walk away, man, and fast before this gets worse.

"What's wrong, Spence, do I make you nervous?"

Without thinking, I stop short, turn, and get right in

her face. "Does this look like I'm nervous?" I ask while grabbing my hard-on. Fuck, what is wrong with me?

My best friend gasps, stepping away from me. Good because I need fucking space.

"Now come on before something stupid happens."

I rush inside, needing to get away from her. Away from us. Away from the fucked up situation neither of us needs to be in.

Lucky for me she's far enough behind that I can ride the elevator alone. I brush my hands through my hair as I will myself to calm down before East sees either of us. That asshole is possessive, and I don't need any extra bullshit in my life.

Unfortunately, I hear the elevator doors ding before I can make it to my place.

"Spence, wait!" she begs, causing me to stop. I allow her to catch up before turning to face her. My reaction out there should not have happened. I should have had more control.

"I'm... I'm sorry. I wasn't thinking clearly. I shouldn't have teased you." She's out of breath as she apologizes.

I sigh as I reach out and rub her chin. I feel just as horrible as she does. "I'm sorry too, it's just I wasn't expecting to be—" Suddenly I'm being yanked backward.

"Do not touch her," East all but yells. It pisses me off because he has no damn clue.

"She's my best friend. What the fuck are you to her?" I get right in the asshole's face. My fists ball at my sides, ready for a fight.

"She's mine," he states with such confidence that it

pisses me off more. Especially after how he has treated her recently.

"Is that so? Last I checked, you treated her like shit and who took her in? That would be me. So back off, Sinclair."

"Why were your hands on her and where the hell is your shirt?"

"That's none of your damn business," I grind, giving him a dose of his own fucking medicine. I step even closer.

"I wonder what Lettie would say about this."

I freeze as the anger nearly boils over. "Her name is Scarlett. She's more than just a stripper. She has a name." I take a step back before I do something regretful and storm into my condo, slamming the door behind me.

Charla can deal with his ass on her own.

I STEW SILENTLY in the comfort of my own room, pacing back and forth. I hate Scarlett's stage name. Fucking hate how that fucker said it without a care about who she actually is. I saw the way Charla looked at me. All the questions she wanted to ask, but did not get the chance to.

What's more is how she looks so fucking much like the woman I'm currently fucking.

Too fucking much.

My mind drifts back to the beach. The way her wet hair fell over her shoulders. The way that tee clung to her wet skin. Charla's vibrant green eyes. All of it. It is way too familiar.

Fuck. I yank at my hair, trying to understand. Could

they be cousins? Doubtful, they come from two very different families. Their lives are the complete opposite of each other. There's no damn way they could be related.

Unless Stefan... no, he would not do something so extreme. He would though, that is the shitty thing.

Looks like I need to do some digging.

Chapter Thirty-One

SCARLETT

"LETTIE," my name comes through the speaker.

It causes me to freeze. Nothing good comes from my name being called through the speaker. Nothing at all.

The girls in the dressing room stop and stare at me.

"Are you going to answer that, Lettie?" Tia asks, snapping me away from my thoughts.

"Uh, yeah." Shaking my head, I walk quickly, I don't keep whoever is waiting,

A shaky finger hits the button. "Yes?"

"You've been requested. Five minutes."

"Yes, sir."

I walk back with a smile on my face. There's only one person it could be requesting me since I just got here.

Spencer.

I was certain that was his fancy car I spotted in the parking lot as I was pulling in to go around back.

My pulse quickens at the thought of dancing for him again. Knowing everything we have already done.

It will be much different than the first dance I gave him.

Much different.

I choose a sexy black mesh body suit. The entire thing is mesh. Even the long sleeves are mesh. It leaves nothing to the imagination.

I add a blood-red garter to my left thigh.

Looking at myself in the mirror, I decide to pin my blonde hair up, allowing just a few loose strands to fall around my face.

I complete my look by painting my lips red. To match the garter of course.

Deciding I need nothing more, I strap on my chunky black heels and head off to the VIP lounge.

Kris is waiting for me the second I exit the dressing room. He is our newest security guard. Short, blonde hair, buzzed. He is nice to look at, but not my type. I have heard the girls whispering about him. According to them, he just got out of the military.

"You're three minutes late. Boss hates late. Lounge two. Get moving."

I don't reply, I simply nod and move my feet as fast as I can. I know Spencer will not care if I'm a few minutes late. However, I am at work and need to maintain some sort of professionalism. At least until I am behind closed doors.

Then I remember there are cameras in there.

Well shit.

When we reach door number two, Kris stops. "I already gave him the run down on the rules. Do you need me to come in with you to give a reminder?"

I bite my bottom lip to hide the smile that threatens to creep through. "No, sir, I should be good. I'll remind him of my rules before I begin. What is my time?"

"Thirty minutes." Kris shrugs. "He claims that's all the time he needs."

My heart practically stops. Thirty minutes? That's all the time he needs? What the hell does that mean?

I plaster on a big smile. "Thanks, I'll page if I need anything."

Without another word, he turns quickly and goes off.

My hand shakily grips the knob. Suddenly I don't feel so confident.

I step in and shut the door before turning to look at Spencer.

When I finally spot him, my mouth drops open.

The man sitting in the chaise lounge with his hands propped behind his head is not Spencer.

Not even close.

"Are you going to say hello, Scarlett, oops I mean Lettie. Surely this is not how you greet paying customers."

Does my boss know he is here? He has to right? Mr. Sinclair knows all. He sees all.

"Well?" he spits, bringing me back to my current reality. A reality I suddenly hate. I hate it more than stripping for a living.

"What do you want, Corey?" I have to keep from grinding my teeth as I say his name.

"What do I want? I am paying for your time. Start dancing. Start stripping."

I swallow thickly and hold my head high as I walk past him to the music player. I will not buckle under this man. No damn way.

I hit shuffle and as soon as I hear Halestorm, I immediately change it. I cannot think of Spencer while I dance for this creep. A song I do not recognize comes on. Works for me.

I sway my hips as I make my way back to Corey. His lying eyes scan my body, liking what he sees. I know this because he sits up taller and adjusts himself.

Gross.

"Come closer, Lettie."

Rolling my eyes, I lean in close, placing my arms on either side of him. My breasts are on display, right in his face. The feeling of Corey's hot breath nearly makes me sick. I feel bile begin to rise and have no choice but to swallow it down and continue on.

"So Lettie, tell me, how was lunch with Kelly?"

I push off and glare at him. "Why are you involving me in your games?"

"Because I can. Keep dancing," he demands, his tone filled with malice.

I do as I'm told. Not like I have much choice.

I turn around and bend over at the waist. I would like to tell him to kiss my ass but I'm afraid he would and more. The second I wiggle my ass I hear him moan. It is so lame and to be honest, it pisses me off as much as it makes me nauseous.

I need to focus because I want answers. I deserve them.

"My turn, why are you here?"

"I have another job I want you to do."

"And just what would that be?" I only ask because I'm curious as to what bullshit he wants me to pull off now. Maybe this time I can give Mr. Sinclair a heads-up.

"I need you to seduce that boss of yours."

I stop dancing and look over my shoulder. This guy cannot be serious.

His eyes tell me he is.

"Why would I do that?"

"Don't worry about the details. Can't you just do as you are told?" Corey huffs in annoyance before waving his hand. "It would appear not. I told you to keep dancing."

Turning my face away from him, I start dancing again. It makes me feel slimy, yet I do it anyway. *How is this my life*, I wonder. How did I get involved in this bullshit drama?

The song finally changes to one I know. "In The Night" by The Weekend. It is a completely different tempo, so I change my moves to go along with it. Bending over one last time before turning around, I decide to ask the question that's been on the tip of my tongue since I laid eyes on Corey.

"I still haven't been paid for the first favor," I say as seductively as I possibly can without throwing up. There is no way in hell I would ever willingly try to seduce this man. Not a chance.

"It will come after this job. One lump sum." Corey chuckles as if he is proud of himself.

I don't find it the slightest bit funny. I needed that money, was counting on it, and he stiffed me. I refuse to let it happen again.

I realize he's not even looking at me when I finally find the courage to look him in the eye. Instead, Corey is fixated on my pussy. His eyes are lust filled. I silently curse myself for wearing this mesh bodysuit. I glance down and sure enough, he has got a hard-on. My moves slow as I shake my head in disgust.

"Where is my money?"

His eyes snap up to mine. Gone is the lust that was there a moment ago. It has been replaced with annoyance, or maybe it is anger I see. I'm not really sure and don't really care.

"You'll get it when you complete this job. Now fucking shut up. I paid for a private dance, and you are ruining it with your mouth."

He leans up and his hands dart out fast, grabbing my ass to pull me closer to him. My own hands fly out, grabbing hold of the chaise. I hit the little button on the back side. Little does he know we have silent alarms all over this room. Multiple on this chaise lounge alone. I hit as many as my fingers touch.

With my pussy now inches from his face, he inhales and smiles. "I bet you are a good fuck."

I try to pull back, but he keeps a tight grip on my ass. I know by the time I am free of his hold, there will be marks. Spencer will not like this. Not one bit.

"Let me go, Corey. This is not allowed."

"I'm paying. I make the rules."

"The fuck you do!" I gasp in relief as I hear Marc's voice. Corey's grip loosens and I quickly step back.

Marc comes up fast, yanking me further away from him. Kris is fast behind him.

"Mr. Sinclair is not going to be happy to see you. I don't know who you think you are, but coming here when you have been told to stay away takes some damn nerve."

"I paid for a private dance. No harm done." Corey laughs like he fits in here, at The Red Society.

He doesn't. Never will.

The minute a man touches a woman without signed consent, all bets are off. You are removed and banned for life. Mr. Sinclair does not play.

More security rushes past me. It is not the first time I have seen creeps thrown out and I am sure it will not be the last.

Marc points to Corey as he walks up to me. "Cuff him and bring him to Sinclair."

Marc wraps a robe around me and nods. "Let's go."

I mimic his moves, nodding. I follow him on shaky legs. One foot in front of the other I tell myself. I don't dare make eye contact with Corey. I fear my boss is going to think I had a part in this. Whenever Corey comes around, I end up in trouble.

As we get to the door, I hear the words, "fake ID and violating a trespassing order."

"Get your things, I'll drive you home."

I look up and smile at Marc. Grateful to be going home. I have no energy for words. I am too caught up on Corey and just how far he was willing to go to see me.

THAT SCARES ME.

Chapter Thirty-Two

SCARLETT

THE LAST TWENTY-SOMETHING hours have gone by in a blur. Once I arrived home, I jumped in the shower and didn't move for what felt like hours. The water had long run cold, and yet I still stood under the cold spray. I prayed it would make me disappear from this shit hand of life I was dealt.

No such luck.

A knock comes at the front door. Let me rephrase that, a pounding comes from the door followed by my name.

I stumble off my bed in hopes to beat my mother to the door, but I'm not fast enough. I halt before rounding the corner. My mother and Spencer are in a heated conversation.

"Who do you think you are pounding and shouting for my daughter," my mother nearly snaps.

I dare a quick peek. My mother has the door wide open with one hand on her hip, the other is holding a cheap beer.

Damn the cold water for not taking me with it down the drain.

"I'm here to see Scarlett and to make sure she is okay."
Spencer sounds unaffected as he replies.

"Yeah, well you can see her when she clocks in at work.
Do her a favor and request a private dance. We need the
money."

My feet move fast. "Mother!" I'm so embarrassed and
can't even muster the courage to look at Spencer. How
ironic considering all the things I've allowed him to do
to me.

"What? I was just telling this stalker to go see you at
work and not to bother you here."

"That's... that's not necessary—"

"I am not a stalker. Tell her, Scarlett." Spencer's voice is
angry, strained even. It makes me feel horrible. What is
worse is the look in his eyes.

"Mother." I put an arm around her to try and lead her
away from Spencer. I need to deescalate the situation before
it gets worse. "He's a friend. It's okay."

She doesn't budge. Instead, she eyes me up and down as
if I am the ugliest thing she has ever seen. "Are you sleeping
around for free? You are losing money by being a slut."

I take a step back. It's as if she just slapped me across the
face. Her words sting as I stand there in complete shock. I
expect to feel a wave of hurt or anger. Neither come. Not
even tears. Maybe I've finally grown numb to her verbal
abuse.

"Scarlett." Spencer's strained voice grabs my attention.
"Pack your things. Now."

I nod slowly, torn between wanting to hurry to pack my
shit and not wanting to leave Spencer alone with my
mother.

"Scarlett! Don't you dare listen to him."

"Mother," I warn, "come back inside." I gesture for her to follow me in hopes that she comes easily.

After staring down Spencer, she huffs but finally comes in, allowing me to shut the door.

"I'll be right out," I mouth to the gorgeous man who looks very angry right now.

I will deal with him soon. First, I need to deal with the woman who gave birth to me.

"You're unbelievable," I state as I walk past her going directly to my room. She follows just like I knew she would.

"Just what do you think you are doing? You aren't leaving with him."

I choose to ignore her as I grab my duffle and start throwing anything and everything into it.

"Scarlett! Did you hear me? You are not leaving with him."

I turn, walking straight up to her. I have had enough. I get right in her face. "I am and there is nothing you can do to stop me."

The stench of beer nearly consumes me.

"Such a slut. It's no wonder there is hardly any money coming in. You are giving it away for free."

Shaking my head, I reach for my wallet and take out a hundred. I shove it right in her face. "Here. Consider this as my parting gift."

"What? You will be coming back. Won't you?" Worry pours from my mother's mouth.

It is pathetic how her behavior changes the second I threaten to leave and not return. She will never change, never see me as anything more than someone who brings in the money to pay the bills and supply her habit. I always wondered if I would be brave enough to walk away.

Today is that day.

"No, Mother, I will not be returning. Sell whatever I leave behind." I continue to stuff what little shit I own into my bag while silently hoping that Spencer's offer still stands.

"You'll come home. You always do."

"Not this time."

I look around once more to make sure I'm not forgetting anything important. There is nothing important here. Nothing at all. Not even happy memories.

The second I slide the duffle up on my shoulder, my mother speaks.

"You really are a slut. A worthless slut."

I choose to ignore her words, but she grabs my arm, stopping me.

"Did you hear what I said?"

"Yes, Mother. Your words cannot hurt me."

In one swift motion her hand lands across my face. Hard.

I stagger back in utter shock. Pain radiates down my face. She has hit me plenty over the years but this time it feels different. Almost freeing.

"Oh, Mother." I shake my head as a sarcastic laugh leaves my lips. She can't hurt me anymore. I will not allow it.

Smiling, I shove past her and walk out of my apartment for what I am hoping will be the last time.

For the first time in my life, I feel different.

I feel free.

It feels good. It's like I can be happy for once. Genuinely happy.

That is until I walk out and see the look on Spencer's face.

Shit.

"Let's go," he demands without another word.

Like the good girl I am, I follow him without question because if he's going to punish me like I think he will. I welcome it. I welcome the pain for it brings me undeniable pleasure.

Chapter Thirty-Three

SPENCER

THE SECOND SCARLETT'S car door closes, I floor it out of the shit parking lot. I have never been so angry. I can practically feel it radiating off of me. Sure, I have been angry at Charla's father, but this is different. Very different. There's a tightening in my chest I have never felt before and I can't explain it.

I need a distraction. One that will not come because I have shit I need to get off my chest.

"You are not going back there. The way she spoke to you. Dammit, Scarlett, if she was a man…" My words trail off, revealing just how pissed off I am.

"I don't want to go back." The words are barely a whisper, yet I hear them.

I half expected her to put up a fight. As feisty as she is, I really expected a fight.

"Good. You deserve better than that."

While I see a faint nod out of the corner of my eye, she says nothing in return.

"You are not a slut. That was uncalled for."

When she still says nothing after a few minutes, I begin to worry. "Scarlett, are you okay?"

She sighs and it is sad. "I will be. I just need to figure out some things."

"What's there to figure out?"

"I guess I need to figure out where I'm going to live for starters. I will have to see exactly how much I have saved."

"Nonsense. You can stay in one of my penthouses."

"What?"

I pull into the parking garage before speaking again. "I own the entire floor. I hate having people around me. Especially people who like to stick their noses where they don't belong. Owning the entire floor was worth it for the privacy."

I shrug as I put the car in park and kill the engine. I look over to Scarlett who looks like she's on the verge of tears.

Grasping her chin between my fingers, I make her look at me. "What can I do to make it better?"

Where the fuck did that come from? I sound like a damn fool who has really fallen for a girl. Either way that sounded pathetic.

"That's really nice of you to offer me a place. I just.. it's just I will never be able to afford a place along the water, yet alone a penthouse. Never."

A lone tear falls down her cheek and I catch it with my thumb.

"Let's not worry about the logistics right now. You have a place to stay, and you are welcome to stay as long as you want."

I don't bother telling her that she will not have a reason to leave. No chance in hell I will let her.

"You've been ignoring my calls. Why?"

"I've had a lot on my mind."

"That's not a good enough excuse."

"I'm not ready to talk about it."

Red flags start to fly. Does she know what I know? Or what I think is possible?

No, there is no way.

I study the woman next to me in the elevator. The sadness I see staring back is all too familiar. It is the same sadness that oozes from Charla's eyes. An odd feeling begins to stir and I have to force it down.

The walk up to my floor is quiet. I decide it is best to leave her alone with her thoughts for a few because once we get to my place. She's mine.

The minute the door shuts, I shove Scarlett against it. I have this overwhelming urge to kiss her. I do just that. Grabbing her by the chin, I move in close. Her hands find my hair and she begins pulling. Between that sensation and the way her body melts into mine as I deepen the kiss, my dick hardens.

Scarlett feels it to because her hands leave my hair and go straight to my pants. She wastes no time springing my dick free. Her soft hands wrap around my shaft as she suddenly drops to her knees.

Hell, if this woman doesn't continue to surprise me. I have met my match. The woman who takes my roughness and owns it like she won a first-place trophy.

Scarlett's green eyes sparkle as she peers up at me between her light eyelashes. She seductively licks her lips, teasing. I swear this woman is testing every bit of restraint I have in my bones. All familiarity flies right out the window.

Her lips barely touch my tip. Very lightly, she places soft kisses before licking it. She even smirks at me as she blows after licking. I am not sure how I just stand there with my hands balled at my sides, not touching her when all I want to do is force my dick into the back of her throat.

Somehow, I do. I just stand there as she licks and blows. It's fucking torture in the most unbelievable way. Yet, I am enjoying it. Loving it.

I try my best to hold out, but the second she engulfs my dick, I thrust all the way until I hit the back of her throat. I hear her gag, yet I don't let up. With my hands now pressed against the door, I fuck Scarlett's beautiful face. I close my eyes, willing myself to burn this image of her into my memory. I want to remember this moment. The moment I own her. I continue thrusting hard over and over. Her mouth feels way too good and I have way too much pent-up energy.

I continue fucking her mouth, even as her eyes water. She never takes her eyes off of me though. Not once. Such a good girl. She takes everything I dish out and she takes it effortlessly.

It doesn't take long for my balls to tighten, and I know I will not last much longer.

My hands leave the wall, fisting her hair. I hold her tightly as my release hits. Her eyes water. She blinks several times as she swallows repeatedly, milking me of every last drop.

When I have no more to give, I release her hair. Scarlett leans back, licking her lips once more before wiping the corner of her mouth with her finger. She then surprises me yet again by putting said finger in her mouth, cleaning off whatever cum was there.

Fuck me.

Pulling her up by the hair, my lips find hers again. The kiss is salty, tasting where my dick had just been. There is urgency in the way her tongue moves against mine.

The air is thick with lust and as much as I want to fuck her right here right now, we can't.

It takes a lot of strength to break our kiss and step back. When I do, the look in Scarlett's eyes has me rethinking that discussion. The fire in her eyes is intense. She wants me. Probably as much as I want her.

Fuck.

Too bad there is a lot of things to discuss. The cards this woman was dealt is anything but a winning hand.

We can fuck later. All night into the early morning. My dick twitches, reminding me to get my shit together.

"We need to talk."

Her face falls instantly, and it makes me feel like an ass.

Cupping her face, "It's nothing to stress over, relax."

Except it might be everything to stress over.

Chapter Thirty-Four
SCARLETT

THE SECOND I'm behind the red doors I sigh in relief and head straight to the dressing rooms.

Spencer is intense. He picked me up yesterday and devoured me, and I mean devoured. I feel him with each step I take. I'm beyond sore, yet would do it all over again.

We talked about me staying in one of his penthouses. I tried to fight him on it, but like all things Spencer, he demanded it and I seem to be glad to do whatever it is he wants. I chose the smallest suite he owned. It was also the furthest away from his door.

Like that matters.

If Spencer's wants me, he gets me. I've already decided.

It's like everything will be okay. There's just one thing lingering. Spencer said we would discuss it later before diving between my legs.

We never did discuss it and it's hanging over my head.

"Lettie, You are wanted in the VIP lounge. Five minutes." Marc's voice comes through the speaker.

That's the last thing I want to hear. I just want to work without any problems tonight.

Walking over, I hit the button. "Are you sure it's for me?"

"Certain. Get moving."

I curse under my breath as I head back to my dressing table for a quick one over. I notice the others glancing my way. Some give me nasty looks.

Fuck them.

My smokey eyes stare back at me. They have no idea the hell I have lived. I pop my lips once. I painted them black tonight. They pair nicely with my deep purple peek-a-boo dress that barely covers my pussy. It's barely covered as is with the matching thong. I also added a lacey black garter set. Strappy black heels finish me off.

I take a deep breath before blowing myself a kiss.

I got this.

I am a professional.

At least I thought I was a professional. Opening the door, I see Spencer sitting in the black leather armchair. All professional thoughts are gone. Poof. Just like that.

He smirks as he looks me up and down. This man who happens to be sexy as sin sits there in a navy button-down and tan khakis. His dark hair is styled perfectly. Not a single strand is out of place.

He is perfect.

"This is Mr. Worthington. He has one hour." Marc closes the door, turning the lock.

I wear a devious smile as I walk up to him. "Hello, I'm Lettie, it's a pleasure—"

"Scarlett. Your name is Scarlett." Spencer cuts me off,

nearly grinding his teeth. His smile is no longer, it's been replaced with a very stern look.

I nod quickly. "I'm Scarlett, it's a pleasure to serve you tonight."

"Would you like a water before we start?"

"Yes, please."

When I return with his water, the smirk is back in place. That makes me slightly nervous. He says nothing so I continue with the basics.

"Do you have any music preferences?"

"Something dark. Play something dark."

"Okay." I so was not expecting that. I turn away and go through the list before settling on one of my favorites.

I hit play and wait for "A Cross and a Girl named Bless" by Evans Blue to come through the speaker. It's not exactly a stripper type of song, but it is one of my favorites and lucky for me I can dance to almost anything.

I start dancing, and quickly find my grove. I straddle his thighs while running my hands through my hair. The movement causes my chest to rise in his face. A complete tease. Yet he does not touch me. His hands grip the armchair tightly as he watches my every move. I feel his hard cock twitch beneath his pants.

I stand up after a few minutes, place both my hands over his, and lean in close. My tits strain against the thin fabric. They are right in his face. So close I can feel his hot, quick breaths. I dip forward and arch my back. It causes my tits to graze his lips. Spencer stays still like the perfect gentleman he is.

I suddenly have an idea. My idea is to break him. Make him touch me.

I pull back just enough and do it again, over, and over until I am all but grinding on him

"Scarlett," Spencer warns.

All it does it turn me on further. I will make this man break.

Dropping to my knees, I eye him. I pull my dress down, exposing my tits to him. Very slowly I stick my tongue out and lick both of my thumbs. I then bring them to my nipples which are begging to be touched. I rub my nipples so slowly it sends a wave of pleasure straight to my core. I feel myself up and down while swaying on my knees.

Spencer's knuckles are now white. I fucking love it.

"Do you want to touch me?" I ask, arching my eyebrow. There is a tic in his jaw as he swallows thickly. I am getting to him. I will make him break. I have to.

The song ends and "You & I" by Prvis starts. I stand and throw my leg up on the chair, just next to his thigh. It gives him a nice view of me and what I guess you can call a thong. There is not much to it. I know he can see my pussy well. I wonder if he can see how wet I am for him.

I continue dancing while watching him. Every few seconds it seems his cock jumps. I grab my tits, kneading them as I throw my head back. My eyes close at the sensation that runs through my body. I do not understand why, but the thrill of what I am doing with Spencer at my place of employment turns me on more.

I have no problem touching myself in front of anyone. It's always been a job. Yet, for some reason, this actually feels intimate. It feels good. Like I'm pleasuring myself for him.

I hear a low growl leave his lips. It causes me to open my

eyes.

Pure lust stares back at me.

"Touch me. I consent," I say the last part because I know I'm being watched. The cameras tell me so.

"Scarlett," is all he says before reaching and grabbing my thighs. He pulls my pussy inches from his face. His teeth graze my thighs before biting down. I nearly scream out from the pain, but he quickly replaces biting with sucking.

My body feels like it is on fire. The things he does. The pain he gives me. The pleasure he gives me. I want it all.

I grip his hair, pulling it hard. All the while I continue dancing.

Spencer stands up abruptly and I almost panic until he speaks.

"I want you to bend over the chair."

I bend over while swaying my ass. He stands close. His cock rubs against my thin dress. It makes me want him inside of me.

I continue moving against him as I slowly hike the barely there material until is hardly covering my ass.

"I consent to you having sex with me."

Ugh, that sounds corny as fuck but again, cameras. I must state it. I want to make sure Mr. Sinclair hears me loud and clear.

"Scarlett, if this goes any further, I will be fucking you. Fucking you hard. Are you sure that's what you want while you are at work? Where that boss of yours can see?"

The thought of being watched sends electricity throughout my body. Just knowing they can see us. It makes this game all the more fun. I pop my ass up higher and turn to look at him. "Fuck me, Spencer, otherwise I'll have to fuck myself."

Is there something wrong with me? Surely normal people do not think like this. Too bad I don't care at this very second.

"Fucking hell, Scarlett." That is all he says before I hear his zipper. He grabs me, spinning me around until I am bent over the leather chair.

I did it. I made him break.

Anticipation flows through my veins as he grips my hips and drives into me hard. His movements are anything but kind. He fucks me with a vengeance, plus knowing we are being watched. I love it. It makes me feel more alive than ever before. I don't know if it is because I am here at work or if it is because I drove him to this breaking point. Neither really matter though because he drives into me over and over and honestly that is all that matters.

I wonder again for a split second if something is wrong for me for enjoying this as much as I am. It is quickly replaced with undeniable pleasure that builds fast. Spencer must know this because he reaches his hand around me and begins toying with my clit.

My legs shake and I explode. Pure ecstasy consumes me.

"Fuck, Scarlett." I hardly hear as he unloads inside of me.

After he pulls out of me, he rights himself. Then he reaches for my barely there dress and pulls in down. Not that it really covers anything, but the gesture is nice. His cum threatening to run down my thighs, not so nice. But at least it was fun.

"Dammit, Scarlett," he says as he runs his hands

through his hair. "This is the last place I would ever want to fuck you. You deserve better. Fuck."

Wait a minute. He is frustrated with the fact that I made him cave and fuck me at my place of employment?

"It's no big deal." I shrug my shoulders. And it is not. Not to me.

"No big deal? Fucking you in the club where you strip is no big deal? Paying for a private dance that turns into fucking. No big deal. I just paid you for sex. It is a very big fucking deal."

When he says it like that, it sounds bad. His words should make me feel dirty. My mother's words come back to haunt me.

Slut.

"You should probably go," I whisper for fear that if I speak, he will hear my voice break.

Spencer shakes his head and walks to the door without even looking at me. He pauses once he reaches the door.

"I will see you when you get off. We have to talk." He sighs before finally turning the knob. Just when he is going to walk out, he turns back to look at me.

"Oh and Scarlett."

"Yeah?"

"That will be the last time you ever give anyone a private dance here."

I'm left standing there, mouth agape, as the door quietly closes.

LIKE A MOTH TO A FLAME, how far will we make it before one of us burns?

Chapter Thirty-Five
SPENCER

Fucking Scarlett back there was not what I had planned. I rush down the stairs two at a time. I need to get out of this place. I don't know what I was thinking. Really, such a stupid idea. I thought it would be fun to pay for a private dance. Let her tease me some. Hell, if I didn't fuck her right there in that lounge. All control went right out that damn red door.

I slap my palm to my forehead. Such a damn idiot.

"Mr. Worthington."

My steps falter at the sound of his voice.

This cannot get any worse.

I don't bother turning toward East Sinclair's voice. I choose to just wait. I already know he has more to say.

"It's interesting seeing you here."

"Is it?" I all but snap while finally meeting his eye. I can't help the attitude. He pisses me off.

"Join me in my office. There's something I want to show you."

Great, he saw us on the cameras. Probably jerked one off too.

Nodding, I follow Scarlett's boss back upstairs.

The walk to his office is short. Quiet even, but I feel the tension and it's about to snap.

East holds the door open and gestures for me to walk in. He shuts the door quietly and walks behind his desk up to the bookcase that is set directly behind it. He grabs a clear bottle off one of the shelves. He sets it on his desk and then reaches for two glasses. He says nothing as he begins pouring the amber liquid into both glasses. I want to tell him not to bother with my shot. I have no damn desire to drink with him.

I don't though.

He slides a glass my way. I don't touch it.

East lifts his glass and holds it up.

"It is no secret that we do not like each other but trust me when I say you are going to want that drink and perhaps several more."

Cocking an eyebrow, I wait for him to elaborate.

He takes a shot and pours another before speaking again.

"Listen, Worthington." He grinds his teeth as he says my name. "Charla's world is about to be rocked. Scarlett's world too. Take the fucking shot."

What the hell is he talking about? This asshole needs to explain himself.

"Start talking," I say as I reach for the glass and bring it to my lips, pausing, not taking the shot.

East pulls open his desk drawer and pulls out a manila

envelope. He sighs as he slides it my way. He shakes his head as he takes the second shot.

Setting my untouched glass back down, I reach for the envelope. I slowly open it and slide the paper out, unsure of what I'm about to find.

As soon as I read the words typed out on the paper, air leaves my lungs. I reach for the glass and down the shot fast. The heat from the whiskey slides down my throat. I welcome the burn. Too bad it can't burn the paper I hold in my hand. What I wouldn't give to just let this entire place burn.

Nodding, I slide the glass to him. "Pour me another."

Fuck, I had my suspicions. I did. I just didn't know how to bring it up to Scarlett. I wanted to discuss the possibility with her.

No need to now.

The bold ink on the thick paper in front of me answers all my questions.

East slides the glass back to me. I shoot it right away.

"Now what?" I ask.

"The reporters will know soon enough. Be there for Charla."

I'm both shocked and pissed. As if this shit predicament can't get worse. He just fucking made it ten times worse.

"You went to the news outlets? Why the fuck would you do that?"

"Payback to Stefan. I am not one to play games with."

He says it like it is no big deal. Except it is a huge deal. This will crush my best friend.

"What about Charla?"

He thinks for a minute before opening his mouth. "She'll hate me for it, however, she'll hate her father more. That I can live with."

He's fucking stupid. She'll hate him all right.

"Did you even think about what this will do to her. She hates reporters, the paparazzi."

"I know so it is imperative that you be there for her. Scarlett too."

Scarlett. Shit. I hadn't even thought about how this would affect her. I stand as rage begins to fill me.

"You're a piece of shit."

East stands, meeting my glare. "I never said I was a saint. I even warned Charla to stay away. She did not and now she is caught in the crossfire."

He grabs the bottle and sticks it back on the bookshelf as if two lives are not about to be turned upside down.

When he turns around he looks me dead in the eye. "You can go. Oh by the way, if you ever fuck Scarlett while she is at work again, I'll have you banned for life."

My hands ball into fists at my sides. It takes everything for me not to fly across his desk to deck him. I swallow thickly. "I didn't come here to fuck her."

"I know. That's what they all say." He smirks and I want nothing more than to wipe it off of his face. I hate the asshole with a passion.

Deciding I better not hit him, I walk toward his door and pause to turn and face him one last time. "You better be prepared to fix shit for Charla. Scarlett too. Your girlfriend's sister should not be stripping at your club."

"Charla isn't my..." East trails off not finishing what he wanted to say.

"Yeah, I figured." I open the door and walk out.

What a fucking dick he is. The man only cares about himself. My feet hit the bottom of the stairs when he calls my name. I turn to see him standing at the top.

"What?"

"She will be transferred to bartending. I will try to fix things with Charla. Just let me know when I am needed." He turns and disappears before I can get a word in. That's not like him. It's not like him. He does not do anything unless it is to benefit him and only him.

I run my hands through my hair as I exit The Red Society. So much shit goes down when I am here and none of it turns out to be good.

It's because of Scarlett.

And there is no way I am staying away from her.

Chapter Thirty-Six

SPENCER

Like East said, reporters would know. The second I stepped into the lobby of our complex, I saw them, it is not like you could miss them. Cameras everywhere. There were so many reporters. Lurking, watching the elevator doors like a hawk in the night looking for its next meal. They want Charla.

She hates reporters, the flashing lights, all of it. She hates being in the limelight.

Such a dick move going to the paparazzi. Part of me understands why he went to them. After all, Charla's father used his power to have East's abusive mother freed. Even still, I don't agree with him doing it and wish it was not happening to Charla, my best friend, and the woman I'm fucking, Scarlett.

I shake my head. What are the fucking chances? It's all I keep asking myself.

Glancing at my phone, she hasn't answered a single text. Her phone is dead. I pace the halls at work. She has yet to come in and I'm getting worried. East said he left her in his bed last night before going to the club. Maybe she is still there. Not likely because Charla is far from one who lays around.

I send another text and wait.

"Spencer?" Scarlett's voice trails from my office.

Yes, I brought her to work with me. I was not leaving her with the vultures. One look at Scarlett and they would know.

"Yeah?"

"It's going to be okay, right?"

Shrugging my shoulders, I run my hands through my hair and try calling Charla again. When it rings, I freeze and will her to answer the damn phone.

"Hey."

"Oh my god, where have you been?! Never mind, are you safe?"

My words come out fast. I can't help it. I've been fucking worried.

"I'm at your place. My phone died while with East last night."

"Thank god! Stay there! Don't leave. I'm on my way."

Scarlett stands. "Do you think that's a good idea?"

"I'm not sure," I say honestly as I kill the call without so much as a goodbye.

"Let's go."

Scarlett nods and follows me without argument.

Good girl.

Standing in the doorway of the suite Scarlett is staying in, I kiss her forehead before pulling away.

"Do not open this door at all. I will be back."

"Okay."

"I'm serious, Scarlett. Do not open this door under any circumstances. Wait for me to return."

"Yeah, yeah, I heard you." She smirks, winking once.

Damn her and her sass. I'll deal with that, but for now I have other things to handle.

When I get to my place, there is almost no sign of Charla. I would have thought she left if it wasn't for hearing her cries.

I push the bathroom door open to find her on the floor next to the toilet.

Fucking hell.

"Shh, it'll be okay," I say as I lift her up and hold her close. "I'm so sorry, Char."

Charla pulls back slightly, looking me in the eyes. "Don't do that. Don't apologize for my father's actions."

I shake my head in understanding. She is right. I should not have to apologize for her father's actions. Stefan had a love child with a stripper. Let me rephrase that. He had twins. He was an up and coming politician who could not have his reputation tarnished. He took one twin and the mother, Scarlett's mother, got the other twin.

Fucked up, right?

"What are you going to do now?" I ask.

"I don't know. I mean, I guess I need to look my sister up. I don't know where to start, like I don't even know her name."

Her words cause me to go rigid. She may hate me for what I already know. Fuck, I am still dumbfounded by the entire situation.

"What?" she asks, lifting her head from my chest.

"What if I told you I found her so to speak." Just saying that makes me feel like shit. I know I should not feel that way, yet I do.

Anger and confusion cross her puffy face as she pulls away from me.

"What? How? Did you know?!"

"Calm down, no, I did not know. Not until the papers released the article." It's only a partial lie. One she does not need to know. It's not important.

"Then how! How do you know my sister, Spence?" Charla raises her voice. She's on the verge of a complete breakdown, and it makes me feel horrible.

Fucking East.

I run my hands through my hair. "I'm sort of dating her."

Cat's out of the bag now.

Before I can register what is happening, Charla jumps up and runs out of the room. I am slow to chase after her. I wasn't expecting her to run. I chase after her even after she hits the elevator door going down as I run up to it. Fuck.

Taking the stairs two at a time, I make it to the ground floor just in time to see her running out of the doors toward the ocean. My pace slows. I watch from a distance as she crashes into the sand. I can see her shoulders rise and fall as she loses it. I take a glance around to make sure no reporters have followed us. When I do not spot any, I turn my attention back to Charla. She is still sobbing. It makes me feel like the worst friend in the world, but I have to remind myself that this isn't my doing.

Her father fucked up.

East fucked up.

I sigh as I take out my cell and call the fucker.

"Is she okay?" are the first words out of his mouth.

"No, now it's time you come to clean this shit up."

"I'm on my way."

I kill the call and decide to keep a close eye on Charla until the asshole arrives.

The second I spot East in the lobby, I wave him over.

"She's right out there, straight ahead." I point to my best friend. She hasn't moved and I know she has to be freezing.

I push two fingers into East's chest. "Fucking fix it."

I don't bother waiting for him to respond. I walk to the elevator. I hope he feels like shit.

Once I hit my floor, I don't check on Scarlett. No, I go to my place and plop down on the couch. I'm not sure why, but guilt consumes me. Even though I didn't know they were sisters. I had no idea at first. It wasn't until recently that I noticed the familiarities and started to wonder. I had been meaning to sit Scarlett down and ask her about her family history. However, after fucking her, it felt ridiculous to ask such things.

I hear my front door open and I immediately stand up.

"Char, look, I'm so sorry."

She says nothing, just shakes her head. She looks like hell.

"I'm going to run her a bath," East nearly snaps, and it makes me want to deck him. I don't of course. The last thing Charla needs is the two of us fighting in front of her.

After pacing for a little while, I decide to check on Scarlett.

Pulling the key out of my front pocket, I unlock the door and walk in quietly. Scarlett is laying on the couch, sleeping.

I'm sure she could use the sleep too. She did not take the news as hard as Charla. Don't get me wrong, there were tears. But nowhere near as bad as Charla's. My girl is strong.

'Hey," I say as I nudge Scarlett's shoulder.

She stirs, blinking a few times.

"How are you?"

"Fine." She sits up, rubbing her eyes. "I mean I don't have much to lose with finding out I have a shitty father."

She has a point. I lean in and kiss her once. "I'm going to order take out to be delivered to you. Do not answer the door until the delivery guy is gone. Watch through the peep hole."

Scarlett nods. That's not good enough for me.

"Do you understand?"

She huffs while rolling her eyes at me. "Yes, Mr. Bossy."

"Better watch it, I may punish you later," I say as I stand.

"I'm looking forward to it."

This woman.

When I get back to my place, the door to the bathroom is still closed. They can't still be in there.

I turn the knob and peek in. East is sitting on the toilet with his head down between his hands. Charla has her head leaned back, eyes closed.

"Did you tell her?" I try to ask quietly.

He better have fucking told her.

"Tell me what?" Charla demands.

She sits up instantly, her tits lift up and out of the

water. East is fast to block my view of her. "Charla, you need to cover yourself."

He didn't fucking tell her.

"She needs to know." I grind my teeth.

"Not right now," East states like it isn't a big deal.

Except it is. He needs to stop dragging this bullshit out.

Charla shoves East. "You're hiding something from me. Tell me now."

I advert my eyes from her very naked body and focus on East. Something passes across his face. I hope it's fucking guilt. He should feel guilty for running to the reporters. He glances at me before focusing on Charla.

"Your twin sister works for me, at The Red Society."

God, when he says it like that.

"Tell her the rest, Sinclair," I demand. Rip the fucking Band-Aid off already.

East shoots daggers my way. He has some nerve being mad at me, and yet I couldn't give a fuck.

"I had DNA collected on you and your sister. She is your fraternal twin."

"And?" she asks, knowing there is more.

"I was the one who sent it into the newspaper. To get back at your father."

Ah, there it is. Finally.

My eyes are trained on my best friend's as I watch horror pass over her features before rage fills her. I refuse to look any lower than her lips.

"Get out. Now," she all but screams.

"Charla—" East stands there, still attempting to cover her naked body.

"No, East, don't you Charla me. GET. OUT. NOW." She shoves at him.

He backs away with his hands held out. "I'll go. I didn't want to hurt you. That was never my intention, I just wanted your father held accountable." East's words ring nothing but truth. I almost want to feel bad for him. Too bad I don't.

"Go away, East. You too, Spencer."

I nod and back out of the doorway. Charla needs space. She needs to be able to process all this shit that was just dumped in her lap.

Once in the living room, East looks at me. For the first time since I have met him, I finally see something in him that I have never seen before.

Vulnerability.

"I never wanted to hurt her."

"You did."

He nods. "I did and I take full responsibility for it. Don't let her take it out on you." Sinclair pauses a beat. "Scarlett is going to need you when you tell her. You're either all in or let me break it to her."

"What makes you think I'm not all in?"

His words annoy me. If this wasn't already a shit show, I would tell him to fuck off and get out of my place.

"Look, we have done things together in the past. Sexual. It was strictly consensual. You see, Scarlett has never had a reliable person in her life. I am the only constant thing she has ever known." He levels his eyes. "So don't bother telling her if you are not going to be there to catch her while she falls apart."

I let out a sarcastic laugh in order to contain my anger.

Of course, the dude would fuck around with his staff. Typical.

"You're one to speak right now. You know that, right?"

"I'm an asshole. That's no secret. I do not claim to be holy. And sure this is hurting Charla right now. But think about Scarlett. To learn that her twin sister has lived a life of luxury and money for the past twenty-four years while she had to learn to strip at the age of sixteen just to survive. Think about that."

I hadn't thought about that, and I hate that he knows Scarlett on a more personal level than I do.

"I'll be there when she falls apart."

"Good. I expect nothing less for her."

With that he turns and walks out of my condo.

Chapter Thirty-Seven

SCARLETT

"You have a sister. A twin." I hear Spencer's words, yet I can't quite process them. It's like he's speaking to me underwater or something.

The man proceeds to tell me that my twin grew up much better than me. I admit that part stings a little bit. Hearing that she grew up in riches while I grew up in rags. To add to the loaded bomb he just dropped, he happens to know my twin. She just happens to be one of his closest friends.

What are the damn odds? It is almost as if I'm living in a dream or maybe a nightmare, depending on how you look at it.

"Say something, Scarlett," he pleads. His face shows nothing but concern for me. It makes my heart skip a beat. Like the man in front of me, the one with stunning green eyes, truly cares for me. I jump up from the couch. Sitting here hearing all of this is making me antsy.

"I have a sister."

It's all I can bring myself to say while I pace the condo.

All these years, I have had a sister. Growing up, my mother never said one word about a sister, let alone a twin. She has mentioned a rich guy here and there in her drunken state. I never really listened though. She was beyond trashed whenever she brought it up. It almost pisses me off to know my mother has kept such a secret from me. The only problem, I don't feel angry. I swear, I must be broken or something.

A calmness comes over me. I feel complete. If that makes sense. I have always felt a part of me was missing. Like a piece to a puzzle, I could never quite find that last piece.

Spencer has just handed over the last piece.

He reaches over, grabbing both of my hands. His vibrant green eyes stare back at me. It's as if he's waiting for me to break.

I won't.

I may have been born to a stripper and grew up dirt poor, but I am far from weak.

"I'm okay, Spencer."

"You can't be okay, not when I just told you that you have a twin sister." He runs his hands nervously through his hair.

Holding my head high, I look him right in the eye. "Spencer, I'm okay, really. Sure it's shocking to learn I have had a sister all this time, however, it's not going to break me. Hell, it might actually heal me. To know I could possibly have someone who is not my mother."

"You have me," he deadpans.

I smile. "I don't know what you see in me or why you chose me, but thank you."

I lean forward, kissing him once on the lips. He grabs

the back of my head the second I go to pull away. His lips find mine once again and he kisses me. The second I feel his tongue, I open for him. As our kiss deepens, the air around us grows hot. My hands find his hair, I tug hard as I climb his lap.

"Scarlett," Spencer growls into my mouth.

I drop my hands and immediately pull my shirt up. I hate having to break our kiss, but it's necessary to remove these damn clothes.

"I need this. Please just let me have this moment."

Spencer watches me, there is a tic in his jaw. He stays completely still as I continue removing my clothing. I shimmy out of my cotton shorts very slowly just to tease him.

"Fucking hell."

I reach for his shirt and he stops me. I raise an eyebrow. The unasked question lingers between us as I stand there completely naked.

"Turn around, bend over the couch."

Those six words have me squeezing my thighs together. The way he talks would be disgusting to most. Not to me though. No. I love it when he tells me what to do.

"So demanding," I say as I wink and turn around. I feel myself growing wet as I wait in anticipation.

The second I hear him unzip his zipper, I bend further and look over my shoulder. He grips his thick cock in his hands.

"I thought I told you to turn around."

"Since when do I listen?" I smile.

He slaps my ass hard. As the pain shocks me, he lines his cock up at my entrance and thrusts straight in. I cry out as the pain collides with pleasure. He moves slowly at first, letting me adjust to his thickness. Not sure I'll ever adjust, but what I do know is I'll always take it. No matter what.

Spencer's hand grabs my hair. He pulls it, forcing my back to arch as I look up at the ceiling. At this angle, he hits me just right.

The things he does to my body is exactly what I crave.

I moan out as he drives deeper, harder. One hand grips my ass. I know he's leaving his mark. My legs begin to tremble and I know it won't be long before I come apart completely.

Without warning, Spencer suddenly shoves my face down on the black leather.

I start to panic at first for fear I won't be able to breathe. It's quickly replaced with something I can't quite explain.

The shaking in my legs grows as I try to scream out his name. He doesn't let up though. Each thrust hits harder than the last. I can't catch my breath.

And just when I think I'm going to pass out, he yanks my head back up by my hair. It's then that I come so hard. I grip the couch as I scream out. What I scream, I have no idea. Blood rushes through my ears as I fall apart in Spencer's arms. He holds me tightly while continuing to fuck me.

Even when I grow limp in his arms, he still fucks me. He fucks me until he finally comes, filling me with every ounce of his cum.

Once he finally finishes, I collapse to the floor with my head resting on the edge of the couch. He kneels down next to me, with his arms around me. He holds me tighter than he ever has before.

Holy shit. That was exciting and almost scary at the same time.

I've never come so hard in my life either. It was pure fucking ecstasy.

After a few minutes of silence, Spencer lifts me into his arms.

"Let's go shower and then we'll talk about meeting your sister."

Reality comes crashing back, popping our perfect sex filled bubble. I hate it. An overwhelming panic starts to takeover. It is as if I can't breathe. Spencer notices and pulls me up on his lap right away. I can feel his semi-erect cock rubbing over my most sensitive spot.

"You will be okay. I'll make sure of it," he whispers. His words are all the confirmation I need before he lifts me just enough for me to slide down on his cock. This time he fucks me gently. He calms me and allows me to take control.

He brings me a comfort I have never known. It makes me feel excited for the first time in my life for what's to come.

Chapter Thirty-Eight

SCARLETT

I TURN THE KNOB SLOWLY. The door opens.

Damn.

Part of me was hoping the door was locked and that I could just get back in the car Spencer loaned me and drive away. Yes, I said loan. I refuse to acknowledge that he bought me an expensive car.

I left my apartment keys behind on purpose but of course the damn door isn't even locked.

So typical.

I walk in and quietly close the door behind me. It feels like forever since I have been here. The rancid smell hits me full force, and I have to cover my mouth and nose before I vomit.

I look around. Beer cans litter the coffee table. I know I didn't leave my mother with that much cash so she must be getting her fix from someone.

"Mother," I call out as I walk into the kitchen. More beer cans are scattered across the counter. There's a trash can not even a foot away for fuck's sake. Use it.

When my mother doesn't respond, I go in search of her. Once upon a time, I hated to go looking for her, for fear I would find her lying face down in her own vomit not breathing.

Not today though. I no longer fear the toxic life my mother has lived my entire life. If she dies, it is on her. She chose this lifestyle. She chose not to change her path.

I peek into her room but don't find her. I turn toward my bedroom and notice the door slightly ajar.

I grow nervous as I walk up and push it open. There on the floor with a bent spoon in her hand lays my mother.

"Mother!" I shout as I rush to her side and lay a hand on her.

She's breathing.

Passed out, but breathing.

I sigh in relief as I shake my head. Why the fuck does she have a spoon in her hand though?

I glance around until my eyes land on my closet. It looks almost unrecognizable. The drywall has been torn up. Pieces are all over the floor. She didn't really use a spoon to do this, did she?

She did. And who knows what else she attempted to use.

Her hands are covered in gray dust, the spoon is covered too.

I can only shake my head.

Sadly, I know exactly what she was doing. She was digging around thinking I had hidden money in my closet.

"Mother." I squat down and shake her gently.

She barely stirs.

Normally I would panic and rush to grab a cup of water to throw on her. Not today.

I walk to the kitchen and grab a cup. Filling it with water, I still feel calm. Yes, I'm going to throw it on her, but only because I want closure. I need it. I deserve it.

Whether or not I'll get it is to be determined.

As soon as I walk back in the room, I toss the water on my mother's face.

She cries out as she rolls onto her back, wiping her face.

I give her a minute to focus or at least attempt to focus and when she finally does she says my name.

"Scarlett?"

"That's me."

She tries to sit up and fails. She is still shit drunk. She'll never change and I have come to the realization that I will never be able to change her. No matter how much I strip, no matter how much money I make. It'll never change my mother's behavior.

What I can do, though, is change mine.

"Here," I say as I grab her arm and help her to a sitting position.

"You're here. Thank god. You can give me—"

"I will not be giving you any cash." I cut her off before she can finish her bullshit sentence. The nerve of her thinking she could wake from a drunken sleep and ask for money.

"I'm going to help you to the bathroom. You need a damn shower."

"But," she goes to say and I hold up a hand, stopping her.

"Just go take a shower. I'll take you to breakfast after."

"Breakfast?"

"Yes, breakfast. We need to talk. Go take a shower."

WE DIDN'T MAKE it to breakfast because my mother was still a mess after her shower. So lunch it is.

I've chosen a nice Italian place on our side of town. One I would have never gone to before because there was no way to afford it. However, now that my eyes have been opened, I know that I am no longer responsible for supplying an addict with money so they can get their fix. I deserve to treat myself to a good meal. Lord knows I've earned it.

It's three thirty in the afternoon and the place is slow. I'm kind of grateful it is only because I don't know how my mother will react when I start asking questions. If I'm being honest, this feels weird, being out to lunch in the middle of the day with my mother. We have never done this before. Hell, I can't even remember a time when we went out to eat at all together.

I WAIT until the waiter has taken our order to start asking questions.

"How have you been?" I ask politely.

"Okay, I suppose. It's been a real struggle without you."

"You mean a real struggle without my money?"

My mother gasps. "Scarlett, that's no way to speak to me."

"I can't say I agree with you. You haven't been a mother

to me in years. You've just been using me. That's not what a mother is supposed to do to a child."

She says nothing, just takes another sip of her water. I refused to let her order anything else. I actually went as far as calling ahead to make sure under no circumstance is she to be served any sort of alcoholic beverage. Call me a bitch, I don't care. She needs a dose of sober.

"Who has been giving you money or buying your beer?"

"Oh, you know, our neighbor."

"No, I don't know our neighbor."

"I've made a new friend since you abandoned me."

"I didn't abandon you." I sigh as I push my blonde hair over my shoulder. "I just refuse to let you use me any longer. I'm your child, not your slave."

I stare at my mother. I don't see any ounce of remorse. The only thing I see is misery. That could be because I refuse to let her order any type of alcohol.

"I have a twin," I say casually.

My statement causes my mother's face to morph, almost as if she saw a ghost. She starts fidgeting with the cream-colored cloth napkin.

"Mother?"

Her hollow eyes meet mine. I wait for her to say something, anything.

She doesn't.

Instead, she reaches for her water and takes a sip. The nerve of her. Flat out ignoring me.

"Mother," I say through clenched teeth. My patience is wearing thin.

"Yes, dear?" she asks as if she never heard my previous statement.

Unable to control my anger, I slam my hand down on the table, causing the silverware to rattle while my mother jumps back in her seat.

"I said, I have a twin. A twin sister. You know, a child you gave birth to?"

Fear fills those hollow eyes of hers as we make eye contact for a split second. She quickly adverts her eyes and looks down at her lap before speaking.

"I know."

Two words. That's all she says. Two fucking words.

It takes everything in me to not reach across the table and slap her.

The server comes up and drops off our soups. I smile, though it is forced. Perfect fucking timing and it feels like forever until he starts to retreat.

As soon as the server is out of earshot, I reach across the table, grabbing my mother's wrist as she lifts the spoon to her mouth. Soup spills all over her lap.

"Dammit, Scarlett, that was hot!"

"I don't give a shit how hot it is. I hope you blister. Start fucking talking." I'm done being nice. I have been nice for way too long.

My mother huffs, setting the spoon down. "It was a secret, dating that man. The rich bastard would come in weekly, sometimes more than once a week. He only requested me. It made me feel good, special."

I notice she doesn't call him my father. Hell, I wouldn't even call him my father right now. I watch her as she stares off into the distance. Her eyes dart around to anywhere except me. She is probably hoping I do not notice the tears threatening to fall.

"Go on."

"Some parts are fuzzy to remember. I've spent the last twenty something years trying to forget." Her words leave her mouth quietly and I think for the first time in my life, I hear sadness in her voice.

"I met him while dancing. He used to flirt and he tipped me well. It soon turned into requests in the lounge. He paid well, but your boss's grandfather was a greedy one."

Sweat beads across her forehead and her hand trembles slightly. I can't be certain that what she is even saying is true, but seeing some sort of emotion gives me hope.

"But?" I want to know what happened next.

"Stefan told me he would pick me up after my shifts. He was offering to pay me cash. Cash that would go directly into my hands and would bypass my boss."

"So a prostitute?"

My mother glares at me. "Call it whatever you want. Stefan had a way with words. He was a charmer and confident."

"How does that involve a pregnancy and twins being separated?"

"If you would wait, I'll get to that," she snaps.

I wave her on.

"That man started showing up more regularly. He made me feel really special. I loved him." My mother sighs as the first tear falls. "Stefan was a popular man. While he loved me in private, he couldn't dare be seen with me in public. I hated it. He said it was the way it had to be. We had to keep us a secret. No one could find out about us.

He had said that when he moved up in his career we could be together. He promised me lies."

Sadness oozes from my mother. I have never seen her sad. No. I only got the drunk and angry version of her.

"I tried really hard. I did, Scarlett. We were together a little over a year when I found out I had gotten pregnant. I was happy at first. That this pregnancy would allow us to be together and that he would stop hiding us." She goes quiet as the server comes up.

So many thoughts run through my mind. *Is she telling the truth? This sounds similar to Spencer and I.* I shake my head at that last thought. Spencer has never tried to hide me. He takes me out all the time.

"When I told Stefan I was pregnant it was like something switched in him. Things changed. He was mad, really mad. He did however, make sure I went to all my appointments and that my health was good. He made me eat healthy foods. All that stuff.

He still hid me away though. I was not allowed to tell a soul that I was having his baby. I went along with it because I thought he was going to make some big announcement. He never did. Instead, I was left alone."

I nod, not daring to say a single word.

"When I delivered you and your sister, I was alone. Stefan did not come. In his place was an attorney with papers. I didn't know what else to do, Scarlett. I was young and very stupid. Once I got you home, reality set in. I would never see him again. He did not love me. I was sad at first but as time went on, I grew angry. I started drinking to forget and now here we are." My mother lets out another long sigh.

She's been holding this deep dark secret in for decades. I want to feel sorry for her. I do, until I remember an important detail. One that she has no idea I know about.

"What about the money?"

I watch as her eyes go wide.

"Mother?"

"I wasted it all," she says without an ounce of regret.

And there it is. The reason I don't feel sorry for the woman sitting in front of me. My anger comes back in full force. Who knew a person could experience a wide range of emotions in such a short period of time?

"I see. That money could have provided us with a decent life. Instead, you were selfish and blew it all because you couldn't get over a breakup."

Reaching into my purse, I pull out my wallet. I flag the server down and hand him a hundred. There isn't a chance in hell that I would dare leave it on the table. My mother is a vulture. She'd scoop in a snatch it up like it was her last meal.

I stand, holding my head high. "Mother, I would say it's been a pleasure having lunch with you, but that would be a lie. While I am glad you finally told me about my father, you should have stayed sober. You should have told me sooner. You should have provided for us. Hell, you had money. But no, you destroyed every possibility of a normal life. You forced me into a life I would never wish on any girl."

I walk away, leaving my mother sitting there. I have nothing more to say, and even if I did, it would not matter.

Words can't change the past.

What I do know is that I can change my path from here on out. No more supporting my mother's bad habits. No more being used.

Spencer has shown me, well practically gave me freedom. Freedom from manipulation and guilt. I feel free.

As soon as I step out of the restaurant, I feel his eyes on me. I glance around until I spot him across the street. Spencer is parked next to the car he gave me. He's leaned up against his car with his arms crossed over his chest. Am I surprised he followed me? No. Should I be concerned about this type of behavior? Also no. I trust those green eyes that stare at me, searching for clues that I haven't been hurt.

Spencer's face is serious as I walk up. I smile to show him I'm okay. And I truly am.

He pushes off his car fast, and envelopes me in a hug. "Are you okay?" The question leaves his mouth in a rush.

I nod. "Yes, everything is okay."

Spencer pulls back and looks at me, clearly studying my face.

"Really, Spencer, I am fine. I got some answers and I'm ready to move forward with my life."

"What about her?" He nods behind me.

I turn around and see my mother standing just outside of the restaurant, looking at us. I feel zero guilt as I turn back around to face the gorgeous man in front of me.

"Today is the first day of my new life. I'm taking control of my life and I'm not looking back." I smile. "And as long as you don't pull the same shit that *Stefan* did, we will be good."

Spencer pulls me back in, gripping my chin. "I'll never

be like that asshole. Do you understand? I am not him."
His emerald eyes are full of fire and honesty. I hate that I
had a brief lapse in judgment.

I lean in close and kiss him. "That's what I thought."

"Let's go," Spencer says as he pulls away. "You will be
punished for thinking that bullshit when we get back
home."

Home. That word never sounded so good.

"I'm looking forward to it." I wink as I walk up to my
fancy car.

Once I climb in and shut the door, I close my eyes.

I'm finally closing the shittest chapter of my life and it
feels so good.

Want more of Scarlett & Spencer

Read a short, but spicy bonus scene from shattered Reality here:

https://BookHip.com/XNFTVQP

Shattered Reality Playlist

A Cross And A Girl Named Blessed - Evans Blue
In The Night - The Weekend
Empty - PVRIS
Like A Villain - Bad Omens
I Don't wanna Talk - Glass Animals
Chills - Mickey Valen, Joey Myron
My Demons - Starlet
Porn Star Dancing - My Darkest Days
Do Not Disturb - Halestorm
Twisted - Keith Sweat
Give Me More - Britney Spears

You can find this playlist by searching Lisamarie Kade Author on Spotify.

Acknowledgments

Thank you to every reader who has given my book a chance. I am forever grateful for you.

Thank you to the bloggers and influencers who share my words. I appreciate you!

To my fellow authors who have turned friends, there are no words except thank you. Thank you not only for your friendship, but also for your guidance.

To my people, you know who you are. Thank you for putting up with me and my crazy during the writing process.

Much love to each and every one of you.

Xoxo,
Lisamarie

About the Author

Lisamarie Kade is a romance author living in the sunshine state with her husband and small army of children.

When not writing, she can be found chasing the kids around or volunteering for one of their many activities.

Lisamarie enjoys chocolate peanut butter cups, music, and reading something steamy while sipping a Truly.